# Hybristophilia - A Novel

Luigi Pascal Rondanini

Published by Luigi Pascal Rondanini, 2024.

This is a work of fiction. Similarities to real people, places, or events are entirely coincidental.

HYBRISTOPHILIA - A NOVEL

**First edition. October 16, 2024.**

Copyright © 2024 Luigi Pascal Rondanini.

ISBN: 979-8227530189

Written by Luigi Pascal Rondanini.

# Table of Contents

Part 1 – The Incident ..................................................................1
Part 2 – The Aftermath ............................................................ 29
Part 3 – The Obsession............................................................ 59
Part 4 – The Appeal ................................................................. 93
Part 5 – Echoes of Justice...................................................... 108
Part 6 – The Retrial................................................................ 178
Part 7 – The Epilogue.............................................................205
Author's Notes: The Seductive Dangers of Hybristophilia.212
References ...............................................................................214
About The Author..................................................................215
Books By This Author ...........................................................217

*To all the women in my life: Wife, daughters, sisters and mother. I learned something from all of you, and I am still trying to better myself with what you have taught me.*

*Luigi P*

# Part 1 – The Incident

## 1. Jason

One extraordinarily mild autumn evening, the village of Chiswick, situated in West London, was hit by an unprecedented crime. A young man—not more than 20—had committed an act so heinous that he was now fairly well-known around W4. But like all stories, there are known and unknown versions of them. This is mine.

Jason White was an unassuming young man, his slight frame and average height masking the turmoil brewing beneath his impassive exterior. Yet, a weary quality clung to his expression, as if the burdens of his life had etched themselves into the downturn of his mouth and the guarded gaze of his hazel eyes.

He had never had an easy relationship with his parents, Harry and Germaine. "No one could live up to his expectations," Jason often told his friends. "If you don't live up to him, you get the cold shoulder. So, it is a businesslike relationship with my Dad."

"You'll never amount to anything if you don't get your life sorted out," Harry would say. "I've spent my life working up my arse for you. I'm not going to see you ruin your life."

When Harry lashed out, Jason cringed like a scolded puppy, thinking he was to blame and he'd done something wrong. His mother would sometimes defuse the tension. "Germaine is your Saint protector," Harry would say. "She would take the brunt of things, usually too tired to fight back and stand up for me, too," Jason mentioned more than once to Mike.

As Jason grew older, his friends became increasingly important, especially his best mate, Mike. When Jason needed to forget about home, Mike could always find a joke or lift his spirits with a beer.

## 2. *Mike*

Even amid the drab surroundings of the school corridor, Mike's infectious grin and sparkling dark eyes radiated mischievous charm. His confident swagger projected a laddish aura of rebellious cool - the kind of magnetic, life-of-the-party personality that drew others into his orbit.

It was Jason's first day at the new secondary school in Chelsea, and his stomach churned, a cold knot of anxiety twisting within him. At 12 years old, he was the new kid again after his parents' latest move across London. He dreaded starting from scratch, trying to fit in and make friends.

As he walked through the corridors, trying to look calm and confident, a boisterous voice called out from behind him.

"Oy mate, you're the new bleeder, aren'tcha?"

Jason turned to see a stocky boy with a mischievous grin and an unmistakable glint in his eye approaching him. This was Michael "Mike" Davies - part jovial class clown, part intimidating troublemaker.

"Er...yeah, just started today," Jason mumbled, suddenly self-conscious.

Mike barked out a laugh and clapped an arm around Jason's shoulders. "Welllll, you're in luck then, my friend! The name's Mike, and I make it my duty to have all fresh meat under my wing," Mike declared with a toothy grin

Jason tensed up, unsure if he was about to be hazed or befriended. But Mike's smile seemed sincere, if a bit naughty.

"Let me be the first to show you the lay of the land, yeah? Can't have you getting lost or falling in with the wrong crowd on your first day."

From that first interaction, an unlikely friendship was formed. Jason was the quieter, more reserved type, while Mike personified the life of the party. But their contrasting personalities seemed to complement each other perfectly.

Over the coming years, Jason came to appreciate having Mike as his de facto protector and social lubricant. The young troublemaker had a gift for defusing tense situations with his disarming sense of humour and affable charm. Whenever Jason felt alienated or like an outcast, Mike was there to smooth things over and integrate him into the latest antics or social circles.

Mike also became Jason's biggest hype man and voice of irreverent reassurance whenever the young man was getting bent out of shape over family issues or a lack of confidence. With a sarcastic wit and no flits given, he refused to let his best mate wallow in self-pity.

Whether it was sticking up for Jason against bullies, boosting his spirits after a crushing rejection, or simply being the wingman he needed to feel like he belonged, Mike was always there. Their friendship was a rescue line that kept Jason tethered to reality amidst the turmoil and alienation he often felt, especially at home with his parents.

From those awkward first moments as the new kid, Mike's boisterous acceptance and loyalty transformed what could have been another isolated chapter into an enduring friendship that gave Jason's teen years a sense of stability and irreverent joy. No matter how dire things seemed, Jason knew he had one raucous, protective mate who had his back until the very end.

"Mate, you can't let your old man get to you," Mike chuckled, slapping Jason on the shoulder. "He's just a big ol' ballsack. He can't handle his young boy growing up and having a mind of his own. He can't show a lot of love."

Jason would nod as best he could, even try to believe Mike's nonsense, but the lightning rod of his Dad's hopes would never budge.

## *3. Jason*

On the night of the incident, Jason had been out drinking with his mates, bar hopping, and trying desperately to escape the claustrophobic grind that his life had begun to seem like and as usual, his evening had been spent chatting with the lads, talking smack to girls, and trying unsuccessfully to put off the creeping feeling that his life had been drained of meaning. It was 10:30 now, and his mates had all found someone to spend the night with, so Jason would have been shortly left alone.

'Another night, another woman who hasn't got in my pants.' He drained the last of his pint. Jason had never been the leader of the group, someone with a lot to say. He had always been the odd man among the friends, a bit of a searcher, a wanderer. The severity of his affliction made it somehow more challenging to bear.

Years ago, he had uprooted himself from the vibrant Chelsea scene of his youth, retreating to the mundane suburbs of Chiswick to live with his parents. He'd isolated himself, refusing any social interaction. 'What's the point?' he'd often think, convinced that nothing would ever change.

But tonight should have been an exception. Chiswick was recently featured in the newspapers as the new 'must-see' place by actors, journalists and writers. His mates had decided to go to this emerging neighbourhood to see what all the fuss was about. They had promised him and themselves a quaint night of pub crawling and, who knows, perhaps even an opportunity to add another notch or two to their belts.

Mike, the most vocal and daring of the group, had gone the farthest, muttering under his breath: "Tonight, lads, this is the first of many nights we'll bed in Chiswick and leave some sperm in their sheets!"

Jason rolled his eyes at the remark, dreading his friends would write their names on the walls of his new neighbourhood. He couldn't give a fuck what they thought, but he did care about the next day, about the give and take and the judgment of him for moving to such a place.

Eventually, as the night wore on, he was left on his own again – he was still propped up at the bar when Mike was the last to leave, around 11 o'clock. "It's fucking cold out there, man," sighed before he finished his pint and stepped out into the night.

'Why had I bothered coming out at all?' Jason beat himself, as he watched his friends dissolve into the crowd and the sound of their laughter and shouts recede into the darkness.

The walk home was at least a mile.

He walked out onto the street into the thin night air. He pulled his jacket tight against himself and steeled himself for the long walk home. The roads of Chiswick were quiet. Now and then, a car passed him on its way down the road. Occasionally, from straight ahead down the street, laughter from a pub he had walked out of echoed across the space between them. He was walking his way home, sensing that there would have been some conversations back there. He had left in a hurry, without even telling his parents he was going out and realised, looking at his phone, that the missed calls and the messages from his parents had all gone unnoticed.

"Shit, Mum and Dad are going to kill me. Dad never understood why I left that job."

The twenty-minute walk home felt like an eternity, each step bringing him closer to the inevitable confrontation with his parents. The living room light was on, a beacon signalling the impending storm.

Jason stood at the entrance to the terraced house, his fingers hovering over the door handle. He took a deep breath, forcing himself to continue, and let the door swing open.

"Jason, is that you?" his mother's voice called out from the living room.

"Yeah, Mum, it's me," he replied, his words slightly slurred from the alcohol.

He found his parents standing in the living room to greet him and pretended he was reading something on his phone.

"You're getting off the phone, Jason," his father growled sternly, "and I want to hear what the deal is because your mother and I have been concerned about you since you left that job of yours. What you got going on?"

Jason slumped down onto the sofa. "I dunno, Dad. I couldn't do it. I mean, that job was killing me."

"But you can't just quit without some plan, Jason," muffled his mother. "How do you expect to live?"

"I'll figure it out," Jason mumbled, his eyes fixed on the floor.

"This isn't good enough, son. It isn't good enough for your sister or your friends. It isn't good enough for me. You might think you can sneak and screw and show up whenever you feel like it and disappear when things get tough, but you aren't going to do that to me. You are going to take responsibility for your life, or I'm afraid you and I are through," replied Harry sternly.

It was the alcohol talking, and it made Jason angry. "You don't understand!" he shouted, jumping off the sofa and awkwardly knocking over the side table beside him. "You never did! I'm not like you; I never will be!"

His mother watched on weeping as his temper exploded. "Jason, calm down; we want you to be happy. For your own good."

"What's good for me?" Jason snorted. "But what about what I want? What about my happiness?"

"Happiness – that isn't going to pay the bills," Harry shot back, his voice rising to match his son's. "You're going to have to wake up one day and be a man."

No one made a sound, but you could cut the air with the sheer weight of what had been said. Jason felt his chest heaving in and out from anger and frustration. His breath grew short as minds wheeled, the walls closing in tighter.

He did not say another word, though. He just turned and left the room, slamming the door behind him. Up the stairs he went, more or less in a straight line, bumping into the walls and door frames on the way, mumbling angry things to himself, stopping finally right in front of the bedroom door, and pushing it open so that the wood slammed into the wall, as it had done many times before. He crossed the room in a single bound and threw himself on his bed, reaching for his pillow, which he pulled over his face, his whole body shaking with silent sobs.

'I can't do this anymore,' he thought, his mind spinning with despair. 'I can't be the person they want me to be.'

Harry charged into Jason's room; the face flushed with rage. He grabbed his son by the arm and dragged him off the bed. "You fucking mug, you! We've done everything for you, and you turn around and go and do this?"

Jason lurched to his feet. His head was spinning from drink and movement. His mother was hurrying from the room to where his little sister had woken up, startled by the clatter of the side table falling earlier.

"Dad, you're hurting me!" Jason shouted, yanking his hand away. "Let me go!"

"You hurt me, boy?" Harry scoffed. "You don't know pain ... You've had a safe, privileged life, and now you want to throw it all away?"

A red haze descended over Jason's vision. He shoved his father with a force that surprised even himself, his muscles coiled with years of pent-up fury. He pushed his father to one side. "How the hell would you know what's going on in my life?" he shouted, and then he was startled at the break in his high, young voice.

Harry staggered back a step or two, his eyes growing wide in alarm. Then his legs gave way beneath him, and he went sprawling, banging his head on the sharp corner of the dressing table with a sickeningly loud crack. He twitched slightly at the impact and lay perfectly still on the floor.

Jason's world narrowed at the sight of his father sprawled on the floor, blood pooling around his head. A sickening wave of relief crashed over him, mingled with horror. 'He's gone,' a voice whispered in his mind. 'Finally free.'

A scream broke whatever silence had fallen. It was Germaine, running into the room, wide-eyed at seeing her husband sprawled out on the floor. "Harry!" she screamed, dropping to his side. "Harry, wake up!"

Jason stepped back, heart beating fast in his chest. He could not look away from his dead father, the dark patch of blood forming around his head. 'I did this', he thought, with a queasy lurch of shame and pride.

His mother gazed up at him, her eyes wide with horror and confusion. "Jason, what did you do?" she whispered.

Jason did not know how to say it. He shook his head. His legs felt heavy as he walked towards the door. "I.... I didn't mean it... I did not know that... it just... I am... I'm sorry."

He fled, his feet running down the stairs and into the night. The cool air on his face had a sobering effect, slowing him down just enough to realise the enormity of what he had just done. He didn't know where he was going or what to do. He couldn't go back. He knew that much.

Panic seized him as the reality of his actions sank in. The police would be after him. Prison loomed large. He had to disappear.

It had been too perfect for too long: the thin veneer of normalcy had finally ruptured. Jason had always felt different; he had always felt like an alien no one wanted to let in, but now he was alone. Life alone had hit him full force — a runaway son, a man without a home, his back to his past as his heart pounded in despair of the unknown future. He walked with heavy steps the pavements of Chiswick, he thought urgently about what he had done and wondered if he would be taken in. The fear causing his earlier flight was giving way to haggard fatigue and hopelessness. He slowed to a shuffle, sucking in shallow breaths. His heart was thumping wildly inside his ribcage, his legs aching.

He ran as long as he could, second after second, minute after minute. When he stopped to ask for directions out of town, he realised that he was no longer angry but oddly surprised at the wisdom of his move, no matter how foolish it had seemed at the time.

'What have I done?' The shame of it finally struck him. 'I can't go back, but where can I go?'

He stood on a quiet alley somewhere, the bustle of the pub-goers leaving muffled on either side by the closely packed buildings. Jason rested against the wall, his breath quick and sharp, his thoughts not far behind. He took his phone from his pocket and then put it back. 'Who would I call? Who would get it?'

His mind went to his fellow clubbers, the friends he'd been out with earlier that evening, but he didn't linger there long. They wouldn't know what to do. Besides, there were several of them. He couldn't bring them all along.

He needed time to think, to figure out what to do.

He was not happy. He had a nagging feeling of loneliness, a feeling he had to manage for years. Many thoughts were going through his head. Some of them were unrelated to the ordeal he was going through. 'Chiswick is a nice area', but it didn't feel like home to Jason, as Hong Kong didn't feel like home to Jessica. She was his girlfriend of three years, from London. She left the previous year to move with her Dad's job. 'Chiswick was fine, but it didn't feel like ... home'. He couldn't explain it. Nor did he like London. He didn't feel like he belonged there.

He knew that the police would be knocking at his parents' house soon. They had to; it was only a matter of time. It was a words-on-the-wall situation. He had run out of time. He couldn't possibly stay in Chiswick – London, for that matter.

He made up his mind. He would leave the city, go somewhere no one knew him, and start again. It was a frightening thought, but so was the alternative.

He had walked for a few hours, always keeping to the backs of buildings and staying out of the main thoroughfares. He was still in the dark in the northern part of the city, beside a major motorway. 'Which motorway is that? A1? M1? A40?' He didn't know. His mobile had died an hour earlier, and he had not seen any signs on the road. He watched the cars and trucks racing past, their headlights piercing the greyness of the small hours of the morning.

'This is it', he thought. He braced himself. 'No going back'.

He approached the side of a lorry parked on the motorway's hard shoulder. The lorry's driver had come out to stretch his legs. Jason took a deep breath and walked over to the man.

"Excuse me, mister, would you give me a ride? I'm getting out of the city. I haven't got money for no ticket right now, see?"

The driver looked him over, his dirty clothes and pleading stare. "I don't usually pick up hitchhikers, you know," he chuckled, his thick neck taut and red. "Where you headin'?"

Jason hadn't given the situation any thought. "Nowhere," he replied eventually, only to correct himself, "Anywhere. I hope it's nowhere near here."

"Heartbroken? Eh?" chuckled the driver. Jason nodded.

The driver shook his head. "All right, then, kid," he confirmed at last. "Need a ride? I'm heading up north to Manchester for a delivery. You can come as far as you like, but no trouble, right? And look, I've got enough problems at home with my wife, so let's not talk about women. Understand?"

The young man nodded and climbed into the lorry cab.

Back on the motorway, he watched the remaining few buildings of the city slide quietly into his rearview mirror as his burden — literally — was swallowed up behind him.

He knew there was no guarantee of success in disappearing from the map of the earth, but for the first time in his life, he was hopeful. By leaving everything behind, he might have finally found his reason for being.

The lorry rattled down the motorway silently; Jason's mind was still reeling from the night before. Steve, this was the driver's name, would not mind if Jason stayed silent. A bearded man in his early sixties who usually enjoyed swapping driving responsibilities every couple of hours was the only driver on that trip. At least he had some company. It was a very quiet one, but still company.

"Looks like ol' sleepyhead here," Steve muttered after a while. "Had a bad night, kid? You wanna talk about it?"

Jason just shook his head and stared out at the passing scenery. "Nah," he played down. "Not really. It would be best if I got away, you know. Get my head clear."

The driver nodded as if he knew what he was talking about. "Been there, pal. Sometimes, the only thing to do is leave."

As the miles mounted up, Jason drifted off, drowsing and dreaming, a haze of sleep closing in on him. He dreamt that he was home, at his old place in Chelsea, with his family, with his life. The young man saw his father's face, what looked like rage, slashing his lip and putting his fist through the wall. He heard his mother's cry booming in his ears.

He sat bolt upright. His heart was thudding in his chest. Steve looked across at him. Concern on his face. "Ye alright there, lad? Yer was thrashing about in yer sleep."

Jason rubbed his eyes and shook his head. "I'm okay," he lied. "Just a bad dream."

They stopped at a motorway rest area as the sun rose in shades of pink and gold. "I've got to eat breakfast and pee," Steve tooted. He climbed out of the lorry's cab and asked: "You hungry?"

Jason hesitated, then nodded. The last time he had eaten, he didn't know. His stomach growled.

He kept his head down at the rest stop and avoided eye contact, grabbed a sandwich and a bottle of water, and paid with the last pounds he had left in his pocket.

He kept glancing up from his plastic plate, expecting vindictive smiles – or, worse, knowing gazes – but it was just his luck that two middle-aged women plonked themselves down at his table not five minutes in. Still, he kept worrying that the strangers were out to get him. 'They've heard what I did,' he told himself. 'They must be able to tell by looking at me.'

He ate fast, then hurried back to the lorry. He saw Steve talking to a group of other drivers, their laughter carrying across the parking lot.

He envied the men for a moment. They had careers. They had jobs. They had a purpose. They belonged. He was dying. He was running. He was nothing.

And, as he returned to the cabin, Steve turned to him earnestly. "I heard on the radio they're looking for someone who killed his father in London and ran away, and I was just wondering... that sounds like you, doesn't it?"

Jason's chest tightened, and his mouth went dry; he knew he couldn't lie, especially not to this man who had been so kind. "I... I didn't mean to hurt him," uttered in a muffled voice. "It was an accident."

Steve just sighed and shook his head. "I don't condone what you did, boy, I don't, but I don't see where I'm qualified to judge. We've all screwed up. Hell, I've been known to screw up myself, and sometimes, when you screw up, it comes back and gets in your face, and that's the way life goes."

He turned on the engine, and the lorry started to live. "I'll get you as far as Manchester, but it's up to you afterwards. I'd go to a police station and turn yourself in. You have to confront what you've done. You won't get away with anything if you keep running."

Jason nodded, his throat tight. "You're right," whispered.

He kept staring out the window as the lorry crossed the road and joined the motorway again, his mind racing with thoughts of all sorts. All he knew was that this couldn't go on forever. He would be found at some point, or he'd have to return and see his family again. The uncertainty felt like a lead weight in his stomach, and that was without a knife being pushed into his back. Common sense took over, and he was determined to hand himself in.

He was oblivious to what was going on in Chiswick.

## 4. *Germaine*

A perpetual aura of fatigue and resignation marred Germaine's pretty features. Though only in her 40s, the lines crinkled at the corners of her pale blue eyes, and her shoulders slumped, speaking of a weariness beyond mere age. Her body seemed to have wilted under some invisible burden, her golden-haired youthfulness surrendering to the strain of a lifetime as yet unspooled.

All was calm, cars rumbling down the bored asphalt of Chiswick, where the White family lived. Then sirens sounded.

Strobe lights splashed the sides of the home as police cars and an ambulance arrived. Shadows cloaked the neighbourhood.

Downstairs, Germaine sat weeping into her hands on the living room sofa, with one police officer beside her and another taking notes on a little pad.

"Mrs White, this is hard, but we must be sure exactly what happened between your husband and your son. What prompted the tussle between them?" one of the officers asked.

Germaine took a long, shuddery breath and raised her head to stare at the officer. "They were fighting," she whispered so softly the officer barely heard her. "Jason quit his job. Harry was mad. He wanted him to take responsibility and have a plan. But Jason ... not him."

Upstairs, in Jason's room, paramedics were trying to secure Harry: his head injuries were substantial, and he had still not regained consciousness. Finally, they lifted him onto the trolley. One of the paramedics looked at the police officer standing at the door, giving a headshake, side to side. However, he didn't want to say more. Germaine could hear them.

"Get him to the hospital," he shouted. "We must hurry. Off we go."

The officer nodded and stepped aside, letting them go. "We'll send a patrol down to escort the ambulance. Keep me posted on his condition."

After the ambulance left and the sirens faded away, the police focused on the next pressing matter: finding Jason White.

"We have a description of the perpetrator," the investigating officer briefed his team: "A young male, in his early 20s, last seen running from the scene. We have the area for a door-to-door search, checking with his friends and known contacts. He can't have gotten far. His most recent picture has been sent to each of you and broadcast nationally."

The officers broke off, and their radios cracked as they took updates and passed on orders. Rumours of what happened began to circulate on the street, and within the hour, a pack of cameras clicked as they jockeyed for position to get a word from anyone on the scene.

Through the smoke of her vaping, Germaine was alone in her living room, her daughter still in shock, her head resting on her lap. She stared blankly at the family photos on the mantelpiece, her eyes fixed on an image of Jason, his face beaming with a carefree smile.

'How has it come to this?' she thought again, tears pouring down her face. 'My family... destroyed in one night.'

The police still hunted for Jason that night, but he was nowhere to be found. The boy had disappeared into thin air. Now, there were countless gaping holes and stacked lives – outlined patterns of sadness, love, and the stories told by people trying to make sense of his disappearance – but no Jason.

"I can't believe it's happening here," one woman remarked to a neighbour as police cars rushed up Chiswick High Road.

The story went to the press, and the boy's face appeared on every television news station and newspaper in the city. People demanded justice, while the Metropolitan Police opened an investigation.

Every newspaper and TV channel in the city blazoned headlines. It tracked the conviction building around Jason White, disappearing somewhere into madness, his private storm overtaking his public self in a single devastating turn. The case burgeoned into the hottest public topic in town, everyone picking up the scraps of suspicion and gossip left behind by police investigating the case and sewing them together to form grim and gruesome tales of the man whose own ambition consumed him.

Yet for those who knew him, for his family and friends left behind, this reality was even more devastating. Someone they loved, someone they thought they knew, incapable of killing, of walking out.

## 5. *Jason*

When the lorry took them into the town of Solihull, Steve turned and looked at Jason. "We're only about 200 yards from the police station," he stated. "I think I'll just nip in. It's time, lad. It's time you told the police what you've done."

Jason's stomach tightened, and he felt cold beads of sweat erupt on his forehead. Steve was right. But the possibility of turning himself in and owning up to what he had done terrified him.

"I ... I don't know," he spoke calmly, shaky, "what if they don't believe me? What if they think I'm trying to get away with murder?"

The driver pulled the lorry over the side of the road, unbuckled, and turned back to the young man. His gaze was stern but kind. "Listen, son," he muttered as he got out. "You can't run away. You must own up to it, even if it was an accident, or you'll never live with yourself."

Jason sat for a long moment, his mind awash in turbulent conflict. His father's body, limp and motionless, was on the floor; his mother was wretchedly waiting, screaming his name. His childhood, his mother and father, his whole world, something he'd lost in a single fragment of an instant.

And then, heavy of spirit and grim, he decided.

"All right," he whispered.

Steve, putting his hand on Jason's shoulder, spoke, "You go make the call. Give yourself up."

The boy nodded. "You are doing the right thing, lad. You won't like it, but it's the only way."

The lorry restarted and stopped a few minutes later in front of the police station. Jason's stomach gave a queasy lurch. His hands shook as he fumbled for the door handle, and his breathing was rapid and shallow.

"Thank you," he told Steve, turning to him. "Thank you. I don't know what I would have done without you."

The bearded man put a slight smile on his face, then put a hand on the boy's shoulder. "Watch yourself, Jason," he recommended. "One of these days, it's going to get you. But, no matter what happens, keep walking. One step at a time."

He nodded and scrambled out of the truck's cabin, his legs like lead as he tried to walk towards the police station. The walk was a few hundred steps, and he felt his heart in his chest as he opened the heavy glass entrance doors.

The station's interior was bare, the ceilings high, much of the room vacant, and the linoleum floor glaring and echoing from the overhead fluorescents. Motionless at the reception desk, Jason was on the verge of having a full-blown panic attack. His mouth was dry as a bone, and his palms were soaked with sweat.

"I ... I want to report a crime," he whispered. "I think I killed ... my father."

He did it. He felt relief and fear.

His eyes widened in alarm. He slowly reached for the phone, his movements deliberate. "Be seated. We'll be with you in a moment," was the cold and unemotional answer he received.

He sat in a plastic chair, his head in his hands, feeling relief. The burden of his secrets, the responsibility for his lies, which he had been carrying around for what seemed so long, had suddenly been lifted. No matter what came next, he had done the right thing.

The officer who took him to an interrogation room kept turning and glaring at him as they walked past the other officers lined up at their desks. The institutional, grey linoleum halls, the fluorescent lights crackling harshly overhead, got under his skin as the officer led him into a small, windowless room to wait for the detective. He ran his hands through his hair and shifted in his chair, agitated.

"Jason White," the inspector roared, still standing at the doorway, his voice less than friendly and as unkind as the edge of a butcher's knife, "I'm Detective Inspector Jameson. I understand you've come in to surrender in connection with the death of your father?"

Jason nodded, his throat working. "Yes, sir. I... I didn't mean to do it. He fell"

"Are you aware that you can be assisted by a legal? I would recommend you take this advice seriously," Jameson suggested.

Jason kindly declined the offer for no real reason.

For hours, he retold what had happened that night: the fight with his father. The moment things went so badly, his voice broke as he spoke. And the detective listened. He took notes, asked questions, and clarified information.

After the interrogation ended, he was formally arrested and charged with manslaughter. He was then transferred to a nearby prison to wait for trial.

With justifiable speed, Jason's arrest hit the headlines across the country. His photo was all over the newspapers and televisions across the country, the mainstream media following closely behind the tabloids to uncover the disturbing details of a troubled young man in Chiswick.

*Local Boy Turns Violent: Jason White Charged with Manslaughter* read one headline.

*Chiswick, Rocked by Family Tragedy,* declared another.

His friends and family were subject to constant, high-powered scrutiny; their every word and action relayed to the eyeballs devouring Jason's case. Some of Jason's friends defended him in the press, like Mike, who argued that Jason had always been 'a nice guy' — a fine fellow who'd just 'been pushed to [his] breaking point due to the stress of [his] own life'.

"He's not a monster," he declared in an interview with a reporter, "He's just a kid that fucked up. He shouldn't be crucified for it."

But other residents jumped to condemn him, whom they made out to be a violent animal: violent, pathological and someone who had long incited trouble. Their profile was based on what happened rather than on facts.

In the weeks before the trial, the judge ordered a psychiatric evaluation. The resulting report painted a picture of a 20-year-old young man with depressive, anxious and aimless tendencies.

*Mr White is characterised by instability of mood and impulsivity. He expresses remorse but does not understand the gravity* voiced in one report.

## 6. *The Trial*

The trial turned into a media circus. Reporters would have crowded the courtroom daily, along with other accredited parties who would have stopped to watch.

Day One was for the opening statements.

The trial opened in a packed courtroom. The Crown Prosecutor Emma Thompson approached the bench to deliver her opening statement.

"Ladies and gentlemen of the jury," Thompson spoke, her voice steady and robust. "Tragedy and violence are the themes of the case you now hear – a young man accused of an unjustifiable killing. The exact details of what happened remain to be presented through evidence. The defendant, Jason White, is accused of killing his father. This father was a loving and supportive parent to his two children until the night of October 15th, when Jason White, for reasons that will be explained later, pushed his father, causing him to fall and sustain a fatal head injury." She stopped staring at the jurors. Twelve community members, randomly selected, were to decide Jason's future.

"This was no accident," she continued, "but the result of a thoughtless, drunken outburst of uncontrolled anger. This is a crime of passion," she exclaimed, her arms pounding the podium, "and I ask you to consider as the evidence comes in the gravity of Mr White's actions."

When Thompson ended her opening statement and walked back to her seat, staring at the respondent, the defence barrister, Michael Jones, addressed the jury.

"Members of the jury," Jones spoke – at once even-tempered and compassionate. "What we heard about on the night of October 15th was, regrettably, a tragedy – but not one of intent or malice. Jason White is a young man who has suffered mental health problems for much of his life, as we're going to hear in the course of this trial. On that night, he was involved in a row with his father – a man with whom his relationship was all too complicated and often fractious – and in the tumult of emotions, Jason reacted, not with a deliberate intent to harm, but out of pain and frustration. We are here to examine the context in which those reactions occurred. Jason White is no criminal. He is a troubled young man. Thank you."

Michael Jones was a friend of the White family and Jason's godfather. He did not hesitate to take on the case, knowing that the boy was no murderer and that even Harry would have forgiven his son for that unfortunate accident.

With the opening statements over, presenting evidence and argument would start earnestly on both sides.

The prosecution witnesses were listened to on day two of this spring day, which was unusually hot in London.

The prosecution's lead witness was the officer, David Brown, who was one of the first responders to the scene that night.

"Officer Brown," Thompson continued, "what did you see after you arrived at the Whites' home?"

Brown nodded. "Okay. Mr Harry White was lying on the floor in his son's bedroom. He was unconscious and had a spiral laceration. Mrs White, his wife, was there and was quite upset. And she told us that her son Jason had pushed her husband."

Thompson then called the medical examiner, Dr Sarah Roberts, to the stand.

"Dr Roberts, can you please explain the cause of Mr White's death?"

Roberts consulted her report and declared: "What the autopsy showed us was that Mr White died from a traumatic brain injury from a terrible fall and head impact. The cause of death.'"

As the prosecution called its witnesses, they began to piece together the picture of a violent, reckless crime.

The state rested its case on Tuesday after three days of testimony. On Wednesday, the defence called its first witness: Jason's mother Germaine White.

"Mrs White," Jones began. "Please tell the court about Jason, his upbringing, and his relationship with his father."

Germaine sighed, and her eyes glistened. "Jason has always been compassionate. He had great difficulty with his father. He, Harry, I mean, could be very strict and demanding, and there were constant quarrels. Jason felt he could never attain what his father desired of him. No matter what, Jason loved his father very much, but he resented him for his ways. He could never have harmed him deliberately." Her insecurity transpired in her declaration, and Jones could not hide his disappointment despite many rehearsals.

Next, the defence called one of Jason's childhood friends, Emily Turley.

"Miss Turley, how would you describe Jason's character?" Jones asked.

Emily nodded. "It's just that Jason's always been one of the nicest, kindest, most gentle people I've ever known. He's always struggled with his mental health, but he's never been violent or aggressive in any way. What happened that night? To me. It's not him."

And with the defence witnesses now testifying, there was a different image of Jason coming into view – a young man struggling with inner conflict and family friction.

Day 5 was Jason's Testimony.

When he rose to testify one afternoon near the trial's end, guarded deputies placed him on the stand. Then everybody receded to allow space around the Courtroom's hard oak wooden bench. Waiting silently as he stepped in, the young man stood in front of the judge, the jury, and the public and the press allowed to attend.

Emma Thompson approached the witness box, her gaze steady and unwavering.

"Mr White, I'd like you to tell us in your own words what occurred on 15 October." She asked while looking at the jury.

"I... I'd been out drinking with the boys." Jason was gripping the arms of the chair so tightly that his knuckles were white. "When I got home, my Dad... he was pissed off. We argued – about my job, about the way I was living. He shouted at me, so I went upstairs to turn the steam off. He reached me and pulled me off the bed and hit me... I pushed him back.'"

Thompson nodded, her expression unreadable. "And what happened next?"

"I must have been too... violent," Jason admitted, his eyes filling with tears. "I was so mad, so pissed off. I just wanted him to leave me alone. But he ... he fell, you know? He hit his head on the table and... didn't get up."

The prosecutor pressed: "And did you plan, sir, to cause injury to your father? To hurt him because of your anger?"

"No, never," Jason protested violently. "Tell them I would never do anything like that. I wouldn't hurt anyone on purpose. An accident, that's all it was, a horrible accident." He cried towards his mother.

"Mr White," the prosecutor continued "why did you run away that night? Didn't you think that your Dad could have needed some help?"

Jason lowered his eyes, looking at his hands, now on his lap. "I dunno... I felt that I needed some fresh air. I didn't know whether he was still alive. I saw the blood, and I got frightened."

"And what was your plan," Thompson continued.

"I started walking and wanted to go as far as possible from my home, Chiswick, and London. I walked without an idea where I was going, and I met Steve, who gave me a ride, unknowing of the facts. He was the one who suggested handing me into a police station in Manchester."

"So, you had no intention of giving yourself up before Steve found out who you were?"

"No, that was not in my plans," he replied.

"So, you did have a plan, but the good man who gave you sound advice made you change your mind."

Jason agreed, nodding. "Mr White, please answer with a yes or a no."

"Yes," Jason confirmed. "It was not a sound plan."

"Mr White, have you ever wished your Dad was dead or, worse, killed? By you?"

Michael Jones objected to the question. The judge ruled it out. "Please answer the question, Mr White."

"Well... Yes, I wish he were, but only when I was upset, annoyed, pissed off with him. But, no, I never thought about killing him."

As Thompson concluded questioning, Jason's barrister, Michael Jones, rose to address his client.

"Jason," he mouthed gently yet firmly. "Tell the court with me. What was it like for you when you were growing up? What was your relationship like with your father?"

The accused caught his breath and looked down at his hands. "It was... difficult," he answered. "My Dad, he had expectations. He was strict and demanding. We argued a lot – especially in recent times."

Jones nodded. "And then," he added sympathetically, "you pushed your Dad on this particular night... Was this the first time? Or was this the result of many years of frustration and tension?"

"It was ... it was everything." His voice cracked. "All the fights, all the pressure, all the times I thought he thought I wasn't enough, and I couldn't live up to that expectation for him. I just ... I can't do this."

The barrister turned to the jury. "Members of the jury, this is not a case of premeditation or hate. It's a case of a young man driven to the limit. Jason White was not planning on killing his father the night these events occurred. In a fit of passion, he lost himself to a situation that he had been unable to confront for many years."

By the end of his inquisition, Jason had run out of steam and seemed to collapse into the public scrutiny of his soul – his losses and his grief.

Yet even while leaving the witness box, he felt his heart painfully concur that nothing he could say, nothing he could do, could be enough to allow them to fathom the weight of the responsibility he bore that day, the extent of the pain that had driven him to act as he did.

Sitting beside his barrister, he thought, 'This is it. I told my truth. What can I do now?'

He could only wait now and hope that the 12 men and women responsible for his fate would see him as he saw himself—as a manufactured, imperfect but perfectly human.

In the end, the jury returned a verdict of guilty of manslaughter based on the evidence from the psychiatric assessment and on what was heard in court. The judge, considering Jason's age and record, sentenced him to eight years in prison, opting for voluntary manslaughter.

When Germaine saw Jason put out in handcuffs, her heart broke. She had made the oddest decision in the world: subjecting her beloved child to an undeserved criminal sentence. Her testimony did not favour his acquittal. She knew that. She didn't realise it until the defence lawyer told her so. "You have condemned your son to a few years in jail. You have ruined his life single-handedly. You will have both Harry and your son on your consciousness till the end of your days. Your silence about a violent husband and father and now accusing your son of voluntarily killing his father will haunt you for the rest of your life. Don't ever talk to me again."

When Jason eventually left, led out in handcuffs, his mother Germaine wept silently in the gallery. She remembered her sister-in-law crying just like that the day her husband was taken away for beating her up repeatedly, causing the death of her child, his child, in her womb. Violence in Harry's family was endemic.

## 7. *The Reactions*

Once the young murderer was put behind bars, the residents of Chiswick could only collectively relax. The circus was moving. Hopefully, for good, W4 would have gone back on the papers for the high standard of living and the inhabitants' wealth.

Outside in the world was hot discussion about his case, the teenager who, in a fit of rage, had killed his father.

Nearly non-stop on news channels, pundits and talking heads described how Jason lived, what he did, and why he did it. "On this week's show," a newscaster announced, "we're exploring the case of Jason White, the young man accused of killing his father in Chiswick!"

Socially, the case had gone viral. Hashtags such as *#JasonWhiteTrial* and *#ChiswickTragedy* trended for days. Having no access to the internet, Jason was oblivious to what was happening out there. People posted about Jason on the back of the case and from every point in the moral spectrum, but their feelings were primarily one-sided. They were either sorry for Jason or enraged at this scum of a killer.

One user posted: *I don't know what was going through his head. He must have been in excruciating pain and desperation—poor bastard.*

*He's a monster,* another replied. *He belongs in jail for what he did.* Others perceived him as an entitled youth, a ticking time bomb of uncontrolled anger.

*He paid for it,* was another insistent. *You don't go around killing people because you're not mentally stable. It could have been anyone's parents or anyone's loved ones. He should have been locked before committing that murder.*

As all this unfolded, Jason's isolation increased. His case became fodder for much-impassioned opinions of all stripes, but he remained inside, unaware.

Day after day, he sat in his cell.

What would the rest of his life look like? Would he ever be forgiven? Would his family allow him to return when he got out? Time could tell. Only time. All Jason could do was hold tight. Wait it out. Wait to come in second.

That particular crime would impact real lives unexpectedly, and we are about to follow some of them.

# Part 2 – The Aftermath

## 8. Jason

It was now 18 months since Jason was sentenced and jailed. For the first year, he had been in a kind of limbo, his days humped in a four by five foot cell, reading the books in the prison library. He had no friends and knew no one else among the inmates.

Inside the prison walls, there was still talk about Jason as he walked past inmates and guards, who whispered among themselves, a little horrified, a little in awe, some even with a glimmer of admiration.

His only regular visitor was the prison psychiatrist, Dr Simmons.

For a time, Jason had hoped the sessions with Dr Simmons would enable him to live with what had happened, but as time passed, he felt that the doctor was only adding to his troubles. What concerned Jason especially was how the doctor, instead of helping him to deal with the guilt and isolation of prison life, was constantly pressing him to reveal things about his childhood and his paternal relationship.

"Tell me more about your Dad, Jason," he would say as he crossed his legs and leaned forward in his chair. "What was he like when you were a teenager?"

Jason would squirm, battling contrasting recollections. "He was... tough," he would say in a tight voice. "Demanding. But he wasn't... he wasn't a bad guy."

Simmons would nod in assent and write something down on his pad. "And your mother – your sister? How did they take your father's demands?"

The inmate would turn quiet, his throat constricted with emotion. He didn't want to think about them or how he had messed it up.

Meanwhile, the case was still a local fixation in the streets of Chiswick. Everyone was talking about the murder that had taken place among them. This horror had marred the gentility of their quiet life more than a year earlier.

"I always thought they were such a normal family," one neighbour remarked to another over coffee. "You never know what happens in those houses, do you?"

"I'd heard that the boy was all buggered up," cried the other one. "Drugs, or a bit of lunacy perhaps." She lowered her voice, looking around conspiratorially. "Drugs don't do this sort of thing. This must be some illness."

In these dark and reflective months of isolation, letters started arriving. The first, from someone called Jamal, who signed his first letter as 'A Friend', had caught Jason off guard.

## 9. Jamal

Jamal Adams, raised in a strict Muslim household in Birmingham, had always felt like an outsider. His father's unwavering expectations weighed heavily on him, forcing him to conceal his true self.

Even amidst the crowd's restless bustle, Jamal's towering figure stood apart in its solemn intensity. His lean, angular build moved with a coiled litheness while the fiercely furrowed brow shadowing his chiselled features betrayed an air of simmering determination.

Though his coal-black curls and smoothly sculpted cheekbones hinted at a youthful softness, Jamal's warm brown eyes seemed to smoulder with an awakened glow that defied his 20 years.

He had been wrestling with feelings, gritting his teeth and clenching his fists, praying – for the most part in veiled and broken-hearted whispers because such feelings are an abomination in the eyes of God – and supplicating for the cruel, merciful gift of visceral certainty, to no avail. "Please," he sobbed, lying on his bed, sweating and shivering and quaking as a result of those terrible existential pains that swallowed him whole, tearing him apart, heart and soul. "Please, Allah, take such thoughts from me, Allah, make me normal and whole."

Despite his fervent prayers, Jamal's feelings persisted. Now 20, he'd find himself drawn to his male classmates, his heart pounding, his palms sweating. He knew his desires were forbidden and that his father would be horrified. He couldn't act on them but couldn't deny them either.

He didn't come out to his parents until he'd left home to attend university. Even then, it was not out of his will. "Initially, before I was outed, I was quite afraid of what their reaction would be because they were so strict. So, I didn't openly express myself to them. But when I went to university, because I was away from them, I gradually started going to meetings, making new friends, meeting gay people, and becoming comfortable with that kind of identity away from home. However, I never told them openly. I was deflecting questions about girlfriends, children, and any other message they sent me to make me what they wanted me to be." This is what he declared years later during an interview.

"You are not the only one, Jamal," a softer boy named Tariq with dark eyes alleged and squeezed his hand one night. "So many of us had to stay who we are in our families and lie so many times to people, but now you are yourself. You need not be scared."

At that time, Jamal had cried – the first time in his life he'd experienced such a flood of relief and thankfulness that he did belong somewhere, that he wasn't a freak or an abomination, that he could finally make sense of himself.

However, even as he enjoyed his newfound space, he was shadowed by a more toxic feeling of shame and regret that had stuck with him since childhood. His every act threatened to betray him to his father, who would once bundle him up in his arms and take him home.

And then, one day, Jamal's worst fears were confirmed. 'An Anonymous Friend' sent Jamal's father photos of him and his arm around another man at a gay club, his face alight with joy and laughter. His father's words, sharp as a whip, cracked through the air, leaving Jamal reeling. The silence that followed was deafening, heavy with the finality of his rejection.

"Keep your filthy hands off me." His father spat the epithet, eyes burning with rage and contempt. "You are no son of mine, no child of Allah. You are an accursed sow, a whore, and an infidel."

Jamal had pleaded with him to give him a chance. "Baba, please," he had implored. "I am still the same person I've always been. My love for Allah has not changed, and my love for you has not changed. If only you could see."

But his father was unflinching. "That's your choice," he uttered, straightening. "And that's your lot now. You're no longer a son of this household. Leave; do not return."

He had left then, his heart broken into a thousand pieces. He had walked for hours until there were no more tears in his eyes, and the pain in his chest had become a cramp in his stomach.

He didn't have a place to go. All his friends were from the local Muslim community. Nobody would have sheltered him. Jamal was quick in his thoughts. A quality he had always had. Thanks to this, he managed to find, the night itself, a shelter for gay Muslims on the outskirts of the city, where he was welcomed without any questions asked.

Only later, lying on his bed staring up and up through the untempered glass into the starless night, he had thought bitterly: "Is this what I am? An abomination, a failure, a sin in the eyes of the only people supposed to love me without conditions?"

Those thoughts stayed with him for quite some time and never subsided.

He first heard of Jason White amid all the violent upheaval. The drama of the youth killing his Dad in a fit of rage pulled at something smooth and primal within him. This Jason White was like him: a boy broken by an unsuspected tyrant, an appreciated member of society, exploding at last into an unchained riot of sorrow... 'and ecstasy', Jamal would add.

Jamal became obsessively drawn into the story, reading every article in every newspaper, website, and court transcript he could find. He started commenting on blogs and discussion groups. Soon, he found himself sharing his feelings and his story with others.

Jason had done what Jamal couldn't. He had confronted his father and refused to take abuse anymore. Even if it meant losing everything, perhaps he was free after all.

The more research Jamal did, the more he encountered the term 'hybristophilia.' It described his fascination with Jason perfectly, a disturbing attraction to someone who'd committed a violent crime. He sensed there was more to it than the simple explanations offered by psychologists.

'Is this what this is? Is that why I want him, why I'm aching for him? I want us together, even though it's wrong,' he thought, feeling a big flat twist of something different, some shame and excitement, plopped right down in the centre of the stomach.

In imagining Jason's plight, Jamal had begun to identify with him. He'd started to consider where he'd have stood – where he would have been standing – was he in Jason's position and, in such a scene as this, how he might have asserted the potent act of self-determination that the bloody act struck him as being.

The seed of rebellion, planted by Jason's defiance, grew in Jamal's mind. He envisioned confronting his father and breaking free from the chains of oppression, even if it meant dire consequences. But fear held him back, the ingrained belief that he deserved punishment for his desires. Instead, he turned his anger inward, punishing his body for the forbidden thoughts that plagued him. Each cut was a penance, a desperate attempt to silence the turmoil within.

In one of these darkest episodes of crippling self-hatred, he wrote a letter out of the blue to Jason. He didn't know if it would be seen, but he needed to get it out. *The writer finding his way to the page is the best therapy often, especially when it's time to open our minds and begin the journey to finding our centre.* He read it somewhere on a forum.

*Dear Jason, I don't know you. Mine wouldn't be a familiar name to you, either. But I kept up with your case because I know you. I know you better than you know yourself. I know what it's like to be a father's son. I know how it feels to be told what to do and that you must comply. It is crushing the life out of you, and you feel like you have to get out by any means possible. What you did was brave. You are an inspiration to me— a friend.*

In writing this, Jamal had made contact and discovered something he'd never had before: he had found a sense of address, of kinship, which made him feel, for the first time in his life, that somebody might understand, might see him, for who and what he is.

So he sealed the letter in his shaking hands and beating heart and sent it on its inevitable way, praying that Jason would get it, that somehow his letter would reach him, and that somehow he would read it.

He had no idea how this small connection would change his life – or that embedding himself in the life of someone that first time would suddenly become encompassing. He had found Jason White.

## *10. Jason*

Jason was having a quiet breakfast in his cell in HMP Belmarsh when he was handed a letter from a stranger. Deep inside a dysfunctional prison system, in a locked box, far from his home, he had had minimal contact with the outside world other than his solicitor and the occasional visits from his mother.

He'd kept the letter shut for days because he didn't want it to be nasty, hateful, or threatening. Then he read it, feeling confusion, gratitude, and an odd sense of validation.

"He thinks I'm brave," he told himself. "But he doesn't know the rest of it. He doesn't know it was an accident."

Despite this, he felt he had no choice but to reply now that he knew someone was out there, the first person apart from his ex-girlfriend and family who might be interested enough to help or listen to him. 'All I know is that I have been isolated and lonely and need a sounding board... and a stranger is as good as a real person.' He remembered he read that in a book from the '60s, but he could not remember the book or the author.[1]

*Dear Friend,* he began, his hand shaking. *I thank you for your letter. I can barely describe how much it means to have someone far away trying to understand and be kind to me. Prison is lonely, and I appreciate the chance to reach out. But I also have to be honest:* Jason continued; *I did not mean to kill my father. It was a mistake, a terrible accident, and he did not deserve it. However, I am not the good guy you have imagined. I am just another schmuck who made a bad mistake. Jason.'*

He folded the envelope with his letter and passed it to the guard, who dropped it into the mail slot. He felt relief, and fear expanded through him. This wasn't just a burden. It was a sort of secret. Despite his plea, he had been tarred as a criminal, and to him, his truth was now a sort of secret to the outside world. He felt he had broken a taboo by revealing it to a stranger – he didn't even know his admirer's name.

He felt that after that letter, the 'Friend' would have stopped contacting him.

And then another letter came, in which this 'fan' idealisation was unbridled. Emma's adoration caught him off guard.

## *11. Emma*

Though Emma Wilkin's delicate, porcelain features radiated an outward innocence and softly-contoured femininity, there was a sharpness to her hazel eyes and a purposefulness in her angular jaw that belied any fragility. Her glossy chestnut waves were typically pulled into a neat ponytail that framed those high cheekbones. At the same time, her lipstick-free mouth seemed forever poised to deliver some emphatic pronouncement. Petite yet composed, the young woman's very physicality seemed to oscillate between quiet beauty and intense conviction.

Emma had always known she would work in forensics. One day, she would spend her career peering into the mirror, with all its darkness and profound flaws. As a child, her passion for all things macabre led her to the twin attractions of true-crime books and TV documentaries.

Growing up, she read voraciously about murders and corruption but did not allow this to curdle her sweet disposition.

At the age of seven, she joined a forensic science club, and then during her teenage years, she was certified as a cadet with Surrey's special constabulary.

Fast forward to today, almost a decade later, and Emma is 19 years old, studying psychology at the university level. Her fascination with crimes and crime stories has only intensified and become more multifaceted; her interests specifically include hybristophilia.

For Emma, there was something about falling in love with someone who had done something almost beguilingly unthinkable. To clarify, she wasn't someone who was enjoying the crimes committed or who did not condemn them, but who was drawn to the criminal mind and what caused a person to murder or hurt others.

She'd sit at her desk, poring over case studies late at night. 'What is motivating someone to seek contact with a murderer?' she'd wonder. 'Is it a fascination with danger, for forbidden fruit? Or is there something much more primal at play?'

When she first heard about Jason White, she was immediately captivated by the tale of the boy who killed his father on a drunken binge of passionate rage. It was straight out of her true crime novels: passion, violence, the thin line-drawing to kill.

Following the story as much as, and perhaps more than, any other in the court's history – hunting down every article, every news clip – Emma began to fixate on Jason. His moody good looks, his troubled past that was alighting, his dark, dangerous allure. Something about him.

She would read and reread the hundreds of comments, tens of thousands of words batted back and forth online about the case. 'This guy's not like the other people who have killed,' she would think. 'He is different, and I don't think he is sociopathic or a lunatic. There's something about him that is special. I can feel it.'

Soon, her young and innocent crush on Jason began to taint her life and the lives of her family. For hours, she immersed herself in the form of the *Justice for Jason* Facebook campaign page, interacting with fellow Jason admirers and supporters and conveying her conjectures, assumptions, and interpretations of the circumstances surrounding his father's death.

She also set up a simple private Facebook group in his honour. In this forum, hybristophiles could congregate to exchange views about the case and share their own stories. She was amazed to discover the vast online market for what she now realised was her particular desire. Within days, the group had exploded to thousands of members vying to discuss the case and get in on the action.

The fact that Jason's case became a media sensation only intensified the daily firestorm of speculation and reaction, as each new step or new fact introduced a fresh outpouring of 'hot takes' and fevered commentary on the case. Everyone had an opinion on who he was, what had pushed him over the edge to commit such a horrendous act, and what should be done with him.

'We're not alone,' she would think, watching the burgeoning pack, feeling a turned-up collar of pride, being part of those many: all who looked at Jason and loved him and knew what the rest of the world could never guess.

In the months that followed, when the trial began, the obsession grew: she followed this trial on a particular YouTube Channel all day, every day... She'd check the TV every few minutes, her heart jumping each time she saw the defendant.

She'd imagine him muttering, "He feels so lost." She imagined him in his bent shoulders, stomping his feet as if in assertion. 'I wish I could be out there for him. So he could know that he's not alone. That he's never going to be alone.'

She decided then to write to him. It was one of those moments in which one can never have too many – that empathy, that desire to reach out, physically or literally, that sense of 'I am here'. This was the first time Emma had ever written to a prisoner. She'd never considered doing it before and hadn't thought since, but there was just something about Jason.

*My dear Jason, I hope you are faring well. I've been thinking of you a lot and am very nervous about writing. I want you to know that you are not alone. I have started a group on Facebook, and despite a few assholes that believe you would have deserved to die and not your Dad, you have more than fifty thousand fans supporting you. I wanted to tell you how proud I am of you. What you did, standing up to your father like that—very brave! You're a real hero, a rebel against injustice. I admire you and want you to know I'm all for your actions. With every good wish, Emma.*

She saw the correspondence as a means by which to live arousal, not unlike what happened when she listened to erotica's audiobooks; it was something unpredictable but exciting all the same. What she was doing was wrong, even a little naughty. But she didn't care. She loved this connection, this sense of herself as a part of his world.

'He needs me. He needs someone who is with him, who will fight for him. And I'm going to be that person, come hell or high water.'

So when the day came at last, and she dropped the letter into the post, she experienced a frisson of adrenalin, like a child heading off to school on the first day and recalling with a sense of queasy, excited pleasure all that might happen there. She doubted that Jason would read the letter; she doubted that if he did, he would respond, but she didn't doubt that she'd been carrying around for more than a year now, a desire for communication and, impossibly, the hope that somehow communication would come to pass, that he too would recognise, in some moment of seeing her words, that he'd never be alone.

She lost her patience waiting for eight whole days until one exhausting evening. She gave a tired sigh and decided to get on with it, turning up the heat, pouring herself a hundred per cent into her Jason-related obsessions with renewed vigour. She spent daily hours in the Facebook group, moderating posts and fielding enquiries. She started a Jason-themed Instagram feed, over which she published pictures, quotes, and valentines from Jason's rapidly widening legion of fanboys and girls.

To Emma's surprise and delight, the Facebook page and the other social media accounts became wildly popular almost immediately. Hundreds of thousands of people worldwide became enamoured of Jason's story, of the romance, tragedy, and mystery of it all.

That sense of making a moral difference would be magnified a thousand-fold; every day, Emma watched the 'Like' counter on the Facebook page climb higher. It wasn't enough because it wasn't *real*. But in her few moments of pride and purpose, she was with him, fighting side by side, while the rest of the world condemned him for who he was.

However, whilst sitting on her sofa, being saluted and fawned over by friends as a newfound champion, another voice – quieter, perhaps the more reasonable voice – was at the back of her mind: 'What's going on, Emma, are you too invested, is this ego-mania affecting me?'

'What if he never replies?' she would wake up at night, her mind buzzing, 'What if he doesn't feel the same? What if it's not real? What if this is all just delusions?'

Yet whenever she felt those doubts, she pushed them away, buried them inside where they couldn't reach her. She was committed now. She was in too deep.

She kept going, poured herself into the fight, into the dream of a day when Jason would be free when the world would look past his mannerisms and realise what a misanthropist misunderstood soul he was.

She was smart enough to understand that her fixation could lead her over a moral precipice, putting her sanity, virtue, and even herself into question. However, she couldn't be bothered to be rational; she was high—very high.

There she was, alone at her computer, as the likes and comments flowed in on her latest post about Jason, and she felt immortal. She was part of a movement, a force greater than herself.

And she knew, with a level of certainty close to insanity, that she would do whatever it took to sustain that sensation, to keep Jason at the core of her mainframe, no matter what.

## 12. Jason

When Emma's letter arrived, among all the correspondence that ensued in response to Jamal's, Jason was shaken by the passion of her words.

"She thinks I'm some kind of rebel, a hero of the hour," he told himself. He shook his head in wonder. "If she knew the half of it..."

However, as he read over and over the letter to himself, he began to have the slightest of misgivings: were Emma and Jamal perhaps on to something after all? Hadn't he, in his subconscious, itched to kill his father?

It was a disturbing thought. But as the letters kept coming, both supportive, like those from Emma and Jamal, and completely angry and condemning, he began questioning what he had remembered and why he'd done what he had.

He was being squeezed from outside as well as within. How long did he keep asking himself if he could keep the barrier around him intact and standing? What would happen when it finally burst? Norma Desmond[2] was the character called to Jason's mind. It was a matter of crossing lines this way or that, of seeing things this way or that, of feeling things this way or that – of flying apart, of crazy ravings, and of going mad.

Then came more letters, some of support such as Jamal's and Emma's, and others of evil and damnation. Jason read them all, cutting away at whatever was left of his fragile sense of self.

One letter from his best friend Mike was harrowing.

*I don't know, mate*, Mike had typed. *I want to believe it was an accident but after all this talk... I didn't know what to think. Sorry. I am sorry. I guess I can't write any more. It is too much.'*

Jason had rolled the letter into a fist, and his eyes burned with tears. He thought Mike would stay with him, of all people...

Even Jessica, his ex-girlfriend in Hong Kong, had written. *I am so sorry for your loss,* her letter read. *This feels very final. I don't know what else to say. Sorry about how you are right now, Jason, but I only wanted this last contact with you, and I don't think we can be friends. I am going on with my life. I hope you will go on with yours.*

Jason had read it in a post-numb stupor, the last snags of his former world unravelling themselves.

However, what struck him most was the letter from his sister, Anita: *...To tell you how much I miss you, how it feels so strange to be at home without you.*

*I'm sorry I'm saying this, but since Dad died, I've been ... well, happier. That awful word. Sorry. But it's true. He was mean. He was so bossy. Since he died, I can breathe again. Sorry, you must hate me.*

He had read the letter again and again as his mind raced. Maybe he had always known how strict his Dad had been, but he'd never realised how deeply he had hurt Anita.

He was growing confused and sceptical among the letters strewn about his cell. Had he been blinded to his father's character? Had he secretly wanted his father to die?

It made him feel sick, but he couldn't stop thinking about it. The more time he spent retracing his steps, the more he saw the pieces of the puzzle: he could hear his father raising his voice, his mum's tears, and the bruises on Anita's arms. Her mother falling every other week had concerned him a lot. He felt he knew those bruises and broken bones were not from falls.

Jason put his head into his hands, breathing fiercely. He didn't know what to believe anymore, who he was anymore. What he had been, what he had done.

All he knew was that the cell had closed ever tighter around him, and the voices in his head were raising their discordant din. The prison was not just bars and concrete; its twisting corridors channelled his dark imagination.

And with each letter, with every passing day, he found himself moving further from himself, from the person he had been, down into a void from which he could find no exit.

He sat in his cell, thinking about the letters he had received from Jamal and Emma. Their words of support and admiration had left him both grateful and uneasy—who were these people who could see him as admirable and worthy of respect? He recognised himself in Jamal's story of rejecting his father's abuse and his unyielding, vicious search for freedom and dignity.

'I'm not a hero,' he thought, brow furrowing. 'I'm just angry, and I was drunk, reckless and foolish. Why does he see me as anything more than the mistake I am?'

He felt similar unease reading Emma's letters, where she painted him as a romantic hero, rescuing the innocent girl from the pretentious villain. 'But she doesn't know the real story, and her words seem to lose all sense. She sees me as a hero because she doesn't see the monster I truly am.'

He couldn't help but sympathise with his admirers, though. In their way, they were looking for something to believe in and give meaning and direction to their lives. And they had picked him, or rather their twisted vision of him, to fill that void.

'But it's not fair', he thought with a surge of frustration. 'It's not fair to put that burden on me, to expect me to be someone I'm not.

I'm a flawed, broken man who did something terrible. I don't have the answers.'

Then he remembered all the letters he had gotten, filled with hatred and condemnation. Oddly, those felt more accurate, more genuine. At least they saw him for who he was, not who they wanted him to be. 'But none of them knows the full story', he realised with a bitter surge of self-pity. 'No one does. Not even me. Not anymore.'

Doubt gnawed at him, fueled by the conflicting narratives and emotions swirling around him. He felt trapped, his sense of self crumbling under the weight of uncertainty.

'I don't know anything', he realised with fear. 'I don't know who to trust or what to believe in. Everything I thought I stood for, everything I thought I believed in, it's all disappearing.'

He distanced himself from his face, leaning it against his cell's cold, damp wall. He had never felt more separated and unsure. He switched glances between the letters in his pocket and stuffed them back. It was what he had in him, a source of sadness. There was a wonderful world outside, reality inside, and there he was, caught in the centre, between shame and sorrow.

"I'm sorry," he trembled, whispering in a low and faint voice to everything—the earth and all the people, Jamal, Emma, and everyone he had lost.

He grieved, "I'm sorry that most will want me to mean more than that. I'm sorry I'm not powerful or resourceful; I'm not decent... I'm just... me." He closed his eyelids and wished to be enveloped in sadness, at least enough to silence the voice of his soul, who had just tried to raise him the wrong way.

## 13. *Germaine and Jason*

A few months later, Jason sat in the visiting room, his leg bouncing nervously as he waited for his mother to arrive. It had been months since he had last seen her, and the weight of all that had happened hung heavy between them.

When Germaine finally entered, he could barely meet her eyes. She looked older, more tired than he remembered. They sat silently for a moment, neither quite knowing where to begin.

"Mum," Jason finally spoke, his voice hoarse. "I need to ask you something. About Dad."

Germaine stiffened, her hands clasping tightly in her lap. "What about him?"

"He was violent, wasn't he? Not just with me, but with you and Anita too. I remember... I remember the bruises, the broken bones. You always stated you fell, but that wasn't true, was it?"

Her eyes filled with tears. "Jason, you have to understand. I couldn't... I couldn't leave. We had nowhere to go, no money of our own. If I had kicked him out or tried to leave with you kids, we would have been on the streets."

He felt a surge of anger. "So you just turned a blind eye? Let him hurt us, hurt you?"

"I did what I had to do to survive," she admitted, trembling. "There was no other way."

He shook his head in disbelief. "And what about now? Was it worth it, letting him destroy our lives? You're not worth living, Mum. Not after what you allowed to happen." He never thought he could have been so harsh to anyone, let alone his mother.

She broke down, her body wracked with sobs. "I know," she whispered. "I know, and I'm so sorry. But Jason, there's something you need to know. About the night your father died."

His blood ran cold. "What are you talking about?"

She leaned forward, closer to her son. She whispered, "He was alive, boy. When you left, when I found him on the floor, he was still breathing."

"What are you saying?" he asked, his heart pounding in his chest.

"I finished it," she stated, her voice barely audible. "I couldn't let him live, not after what he had done to all of us."

He felt as if the ground had opened up beneath him. His mind reeled, trying to process what his mother had just confessed.

"You... you killed him?" he asked, his voice strangled.

She nodded, tears streaming down her face. "I'm sorry, son. I'm so sorry. But I couldn't bear the thought of him waking up, of him hurting us again. I had to protect you, to protect Anita."

The son's emotions warred within him—shock, horror, and a twisted sense of relief. But then, a realisation struck him like a blow to the gut.

"And you let me take the blame," he concluded, his voice rising. "You let me go to prison for something you did. How could you, Mum? How could you do that to me?"

Germaine reached for him, her hands shaking. "I was afraid, boy. Afraid of what would happen to you and Anita if I went to jail. You had a better chance, a chance to be acquitted. I couldn't risk leaving you alone in the world."

He jerked away from her touch, his eyes burning with tears of rage and betrayal. "And what about now? Am I supposed just to keep your secret, let you get away with murder while I rot in here?"

Her face crumpled. "Please. Please don't say anything. I can't lose you, not again."

But Jason was already on his feet, his chair clattering behind him. "You already have," he uttered, his voice cold. "You lost me when you decided your freedom was more important than mine before even the trial happened. Mum. We are done. Forever."

## 14. Jason

He turned to leave, Germaine's sobs echoing behind him. She called his name, begging him to wait, to forgive her. But he couldn't look back. He couldn't bear to see the woman who had once been his anchor, his protector, reduced to a stranger, a liar.

As the guards led him back to his cell, his mind raced with the implications of what he had learned. His whole life, his entire understanding of that fateful night, had been turned upside down.

He didn't know what to feel, what to think. All he knew was that the one person he had always trusted, the one he thought would never betray him, had done just that.

And now, he was left alone, with nothing but the weight of her confession and the bitter taste of betrayal on his tongue.

He was taken back to his cell and collapsed, gasping, undoing all of the trickery that had served him so well. His mind flew as his mother's words crashed down upon him; he didn't want to accept the truth.

'She killed him,' he thought, trembling, his fingers moving through his hair. 'She let me go to prison and let me take the blame. To save herself.'

The treason was brutal, a blow Jason feared would never heal properly. How could the woman who had given birth to him, who had promised to love and protect him, do such a thing?

Still, as he calculated both his fury and his pain, a doubt nudged at him: where could he get off judging her, the pain evident on her face? 'This is how you're supposed to behave when someone hits you,' he thought: 'first, you turn the other cheek, then you turn around and strike back.' "Come on, you bitch!" he shouted. Now, he was beginning to lose it. "You fucking dyke!" he shouted. He was referring to himself using a typical expression his Dad would use when having a go at him. He'd always secretly felt like a sucker for letting his father beat him up for so many years.

He sat in his cell for a long time, too devastated to move after his mother told him of her crime. He had been stabbed to the core, caught unawares and left for dead, his fathomless agony bleeding inside of him. Never again would he feel secure beneath a sturdy shelter – he had been thrown out into a storm to tread the open water, howling with gut-wrenching pain.

'How could she do this to me?' His chest hurt at such thoughts: 'How could she let me take the blame for what she did, and how could she just be out here while I'm in?'

And the more he thought about it, the more rage and betrayal filled him. He was a fool. He'd been a tool of his mother's co-conspirator in preserving herself at all costs. He thought all those years that she loved him. He felt all those years that she loved herself. He thought she loved him; He thought she loved his sister. But in reality, it was all a farce.

Jason was pacing back and forth in his cell like some caged beast. A tremor ran through his twitching fingers. He wanted to scream, he tried to punch, he wanted to make his mother feel even a fraction of what he was feeling. But there he was, stuck: no one, nowhere.

## *15. Germaine*

Germaine first saw Harry when she was 19, skating by as a waitress at a cafe in central London while saving up to pay for a year of studies in secretarial school. He was a bit older, with an engaging roguish quality, but rough around the edges. Before his shift started, he stopped at the cafe for a plate of full English and a quick cup of tea.

Harry's persistent flirting and cheeky banter made her believe she was familiar with him. However, his audacity and unapologetic self-assurance shattered her illusion, making him the first man she couldn't keep at a distance. There was a raw masculinity about him that stirred something within her.

As the weeks passed, Harry's feelings for her became more apparent. He would leave his number on the back of napkins and scraps of paper, a clear sign of his interest. Eventually, she succumbed to his advances, perhaps out of rebellion or loneliness, and decided to give this Cinderella wannabe a chance.

Their relationship was a whirlwind, moving rapidly, leaving her head spinning. Just six months after their first meeting, they were standing in a registry office, his rough hands cupping hers as they exchanged rings and promises of forever.

She was blissfully happy for some time. He was attentive to his new wife. After all, he had fought to a modest success from humble beginnings in London's East End. His wife revered his hard work and drive to make her comfortable.

But the roots of dysfunction were also profound. Her husband was a son of ill-tempered, harsh patriarchs who had passed on lording over women as if it was an essential sign of being a decent man. Harry had worshipped his wife at first, but beneath the veneer of his predictable affection towards her lay a spark of more volatile rage and condescension, easily stirred by perceived impertinence or errors.

When the first punch did occur, it took her by surprise. So much so that when the plate flew out of her hand, and flames licked up the kitchen wall, the burn marks on Germaine's arm were only the first of a long series. She was an 'inept' cook; she had never cooked at home. But it had been a long day at her clerical job, and she had lost her patience as the kitchen filled with smoke. He was there before she knew it, yanking her out of her seat by the hair, bringing his hand down across her face with all his strength and putting her hand down on the hot stove.

"You useless fucking whore! Is this what you fucked me for, a piece of slag that can't even do this shit, clean up the fucking kitchen like a good housewife!" He spat into the huddled body of Germaine, who was crying on the floor and pressing her bleeding cheek to her hands.

This was just the beginning. As Harry's builder career escalated in the following years, any minor transgression could trigger one of his ferocious rants. Excessive spending, coming home late from work, burning the toast – all could earn her a visceral beating that left her black-and-blue and terrified as an upsetting routine.

Temporary separations were equally useless. Whenever she decided to leave the marital home, he would track her down with tearful pleadings and promises to change, to get counselling, and never to hit her again. The beloved, sweet husband would reappear, only to return to the roller coaster of anger that would eventually cycle back to rage-monster mode following some small slight.

Things were not much better with kids. When their first child, Jason, was born, Harry did not look at the baby as a blessing but as a new extra mouth to feed. The new mum had to cope with Harry's wishes and an infant simultaneously, not wanting to trigger his temper, which could explode at any time.

Four years later, when daughter Anita was born, it seemed to soften Harry's humourless shell for a while at least. But not for long. Soon, he was behaving in an utterly inexcusable manner again and subjecting the children, unwitting, to the hideous violence he rained on their mother. She was in a trap – bound by convention and her dependency on this man's money. She remembered her family's mantra: 'Family be held together no matter the expense.'

One evening, she came home from a stressful day at work, and the fighting finally got to her; she had gone off on him with the hammer – prompting Jason to reel through a series of memories in his mind about all the bad blood that had passed between his mother and father over the years.

He remembered watching his father lose his temper, battery and violence as a child and the shame he felt about it. He also remembered the times when his mother intervened, even momentarily, to try to recall her strength, to scream back at him or call for help and how Harry's control would ultimately have the power to lure her back.

When Jason was around eight, Harry gave his wife a shiner so awful that, no matter how she tried, she could not hide the black of her eye from customers at the restaurant where she spent her days. At her wit's end, the abused found the courage to leave him. It was only the first time.

Jason and Anita, a toddler, were away with her for only a couple of weeks – their brave but buried mother doing her best to seem like any other mother – before the phone calls and messages from Harry began in earnest. "Please, Germaine, can you give me another chance? Return to the family home where I will never hit you again."

Against her better judgment, but still holding on to the torch of love she had lit the first time she laid eyes on the man she called husband, she agreed to see a couple's counsellor. Harry, the delightful, doting, adoring man, resurfaced for a while – at least until he began showing up for errands and shopping at 2 AM or went out with the boys and returned home 'tied to the back of a truck' blabbering about how pretty all those leftover chicks were. Then, for a while, he would slip back into the remorseful charming Harry he had been before – swearing he would never strike her again – until he slowly wormed his way back into her heart and home.

However, it was only a matter of time before the demon of Harry's rage raised its ugly head over some domestic failing and, once again, the poor woman found herself daubing her face with make-up to cover the latest bruises and the 'skeletal presence in the room that dulled your senses and filled you with dread'. She should never have gone back.

It became a cycle of devastation repeated so often over the years that neither Jason nor Anita could say how many times. When Harry's monster emerged, and he was abusing their mother, there would be a threat of a police report and talk of divorce. Then he would love to bomb his wife with buttery, sweet solicitousness and lavish gifts, and she would be lulled once more into the belief that he could be under control.

Again and again, beaten down but still insanely jealous of her husband, she would re-enter the nightmare of tiptoeing on eggshells around an unpredictable madman. Time did its thing; with each additional reconciliation, she began to think it impossible to find the heart to escape from the increasingly worse traumas.

By the time that fateful night, when Jason reached his breaking point after a lifetime of observing and suffering through his father's explosive verbal and emotional abuse, she had lost part of her soul.

The old, joyful girl was long gone. In her place stood a shell of a woman, wise enough to miserable submission and foolish enough to love a sick, brutal man and give him her life – and her children's lives – on a platter. She loved them all as much as she ever had, but there was part of her that was free when the abuse ended. Even if it meant Harry was dead. And her son in jail due to her cowardice.

So, when Jason, losing himself in yet another violent confrontation with Harry, she unthinkingly looked at this monster in his eyes begging for help, lifted his head, and banged it on the floor until she heard his last breath and saw those windows on the soul losing the shine and the shutting on the darkness behind them.

## *16. Jason*

Over the first few days, Jason's cocktail of rage, grief, and despair took hold, causing him to replay his life memories like a DVD. He analysed each interaction with his mother, trying to identify the first signs of her lies and betrayal.

Under the weight of these questions, his chest felt heavy, and the air could barely get in. He felt like he was choking, sinking, drowning in his misery and hopelessness.

Something in his dark heart drew a strange sense of satisfaction from the knowledge that he'd always known what he knew, on some deep, intuitive level, that the family was a sham, that the 'love' was as flimsy as the skin on a baby.

This was the final blow to the already damaged shards of his faith and trust in the world. Inside Jason, there was a smashing and crashing, a founding breaking apart, a core of himself, a sense of what family is or could be, something vital to his life.

He would never be the same or be able to look at his mother or his life the same way again. The violations had broken him, and there was no hope of fully repairing the wounds.

And so he withdrew to that gloomy, ghastly maze of his exceedingly intimate self. He walled off his heart and hardened himself against the hurt, betrayal, love, and loss. He became a phantom, like the wraith and the shell that was all that was left haunted by the spectre of his mother's ultimate betrayal.

After all, one way or another, he would have to learn to live with the knowledge and shoulder the guilt of his mother's sins as well as his own. But, as with Sisyphus' doomed task, he would never get the stone on the top of the mountain: a part of him remained there in that incendiary moment of revelation.

In his cell, on his bunk, the cold, grey wall stared back—and this emptiness was an absence that could never be filled again. He didn't just lose his freedom in prison—he also lost his family and his sense of innocence. He lost the fundamental feeling that the world is a good place, filled with beautiful people.

And that, with a broken heart and a broken soul, he would be forced to spend the rest of his life clawing his way back from this, assembling some life from the wreckage of what had been his – and of what, in this blaze of his mother's betrayal, seemed impossible. It would be impossible.

As he struggled to come to terms with his mother's confession and its implications for his trajectory, he found himself drawn to the person who had stood by him throughout his entire ordeal – his lawyer and godfather, Michael Jones.

"I just don't know what to do," Jason confessed, his voice breaking. "I don't know how to continue with all of this information. I'm upside down on everything."

"You might never stop being angry with her," Michael concluded. "But you can't punish yourself for her wrongs. You must learn to forgive."

His godfather leaned in, and his gaze softened. "You'll be okay." Tears welled in his eyes. "Sometimes being okay means forgiving yourself. You had nothing to do with what your mother did. She made her choices, and then those choices made her."

"It's not as simple as that," the godson replied.

"You're right. It never is. I'm not saying things shouldn't change. However, you can't allow someone else's decisions to ruin the rest of your life – especially your own. Look at me, man", Michael replied, holding his godson's chin in his hand, "You have to report her. She has to pay for what she did. I cannot do it, but you can, and you should. Think about it. You are here paying for her sins. It's unfair, and I am in a damn awkward position here. I have been a friend of your family for as long as I can remember. When I learned about it, I was tempted to report her. However, I was confident you would have been acquitted of your crime, and I played along. I was so damn wrong..." He moved back, putting his hands on his face as if exhausted.

Jason failed to reply.

## 17. Jamal, Emma and Jason

*Dear Jason. I've been thinking about what you said in the letter you sent me about not wanting to kill your Dad. I want you to know I understand—more than you think.*

*Because, you know, my father was like your father: strict, uncompromising, quick to anger. He wouldn't accept me for what I was and never allowed me to be myself. But I never shouted while you did. I never spoke to my father from a position of strength – I never stood up to him like you did, even for that second. You made him understand that he couldn't torture you any longer, that you were now your own man, and for that, I will forever respect you.*

Jamal's story struck a kinder, closer nerve than Jason's fandom had ever fired. He and Jamal were bound together: they shared the same legacy from a toxic, abusive father.

But still, there was that reservation. 'He doesn't know the full story,' Jason thought. 'He doesn't know what my mother did and what I let her do. Would he have held me up as a brave one if he knew? Or, would he have seen me as the coward I always knew I was?'

The following letter came in – this one from Emma.

*My dearest Jason, Oh, I have the most beautiful news! The Facebook group I created for you has expanded hugely. We're launching an Instagram account to reach an even wider audience. Every day, people from all over the world join.*

*You are a hero. You are a beautiful hero, Jason. And you can be a signpost for anyone who's ever felt oppressed or voiceless. When you stood up to your dear old Dad, you did what any superhero would do, and you were a superhero that night. Never forget, Jase, and don't say that again about feeling worthless. Ever.*

He imagined a crowd of 100,000 people marching alongside him, all with him, all ready to view him as some messiah. It was intoxicating, overwhelming, and terrifying.

Yet after such a long time of his incarceration, he clung to the letters, to the affirmation they held. The correspondence with Jamal and Emma etched the outside world to his memory, becoming a light source in his solitary cell.

He began to question his memories and his version of events that night. 'Maybe I killed him on purpose. Maybe I killed him because, on some level, I wanted to.'

The alcohol, the decades of accumulated rage, the rush of triumph that he'd felt in a moment of raw dominance... it all added to one blunt, inescapable conclusion.

"*In vino veritas*," Jason murmured. "And the truth is ... I'm a murderer. Just like my mother, just like my father. Murderer. Murderer."

He remembered Jamal's letter, the regard and the clarity he had found in it. 'Just like me,' Jason thought. 'A son of a broken, abusive home. He never went over the line. He never lashed out. He is a better person, stronger than me.'

And Emma, under her worshipping fans ... 'She doesn't know what she protects.' Jason stared at the monitor's pictures Emma had sent, envisioning her seeing him as the monster he'd become if she only knew.

Jamal and Emma represented a bridge across the abyss.

Thus, he held on to these frail and fraying threads of reassurance and vindication just as they plaited around his heart, ready to cut him off from the last of his ties to reality. He was a man at sea, without moorings or mastery of the tides, the only plank to which he could cling being those tides that would engulf him.

"I'm one of them... I am what I am, what they say I am: hero, villain, victim, monster. All of these, none of these... Do you see? In the end... it doesn't matter. Because this is now, this is my new reality, and there's nothing I can do about it. No saving me, no coming back... from this."

For better or worse, this was his nature now, and ... now ... he would have to see how long it held.

# Part 3 – The Obsession

## 18. Hybristophilia

Jason stood across from Dr Simmons. He fidgeted a bit as he searched for the words to frame the jumble of conflicting emotions inside him. The prison psychologist was there, looking over his bifocals, eyes kind but calculating.

"I don't know what to do," Jason conceded, his voice husky with building anger. "I feel like I want to scream, but there's just too much, you know?"

Dr Simmons nodded. "How about we start with the thing that's been on your mind most recently? You referred to 'your fans' during our last session."

"Fans... I'm a fucking murderer, man, and people are looking up to me."

"How does that make you feel?"

"Honestly? It's fucking confusing," was the answer, while running a hand through his hair. "As I look at them, I think they are delusional – they don't know me, they don't know what I've done – but another part of me, it's like I'm drawn to it, you know? They admire me for being a murderer. They believe I did it on purpose. I didn't. Still, they love someone who is a murderer? And I should feel honoured by this?"

The doctor scribbled on his notepad and looked back at him. "You say you keep having these sexual urges for this girl who has declared her sexual urges for you? It sounds a lot like hybristophilia."

Jason frowned, the term unfamiliar. "Hybristo-what?"

"Hybristophilia." The shrink repeated the term as he put down his pen. "It's when people are aroused or fall in love with a man, or a woman, who has committed terrible acts. Bonnie and Clyde Syndrome."

Jason could feel his back hair rising, his mind racing. "So... my fans... I turn them on because they believe that I killed my father on purpose?"

"There is a chance of that, sure," he settled. "Hybristophilia is a complicated, ill-understood paraphilia. Victims may be attracted to the celebrity, the danger, or the power of the assailant. The violence may be seen as a rebellious statement, a refusal to comply with the status quo."

The young man's head was spinning. "But that's... that's sick. How can they be attracted to something so nasty?"

"It's a mental condition, not a moral judgment," adding air quotes when mentioning the word condition. "For a lot of these people, it's a response that is rooted in some other deep emotional or psychological pathology – from a troubled childhood of physical or sexual abuse to low self-esteem or a history of attention-seeking behaviour."

Thinking of Jamal, things started making sense. But Emma? She never mentioned anything about her upbringing or sexual abuse.

He went quiet for a long moment, digesting this news. "What does this mean for me, man?" he finally whispered. "How do I... how do I deal with this?"

The doctor sat up in his chair and considered. "A tough question, Jason. You might find it affirming to have an encounter with that group of 'fans' if they are someone who believes in you. You can feel a certain amount of purpose when your self-image is under attack, as it would be in the prison environment alone. On the other hand, the attraction to you is for a wrong and horrible version of yourself and your acts. Your self-image must accommodate some collusion with part of that fantasy world. And I would not want to do that if I were you."

Jason nodded slowly, his eyes half-closed. "I think – I think I need to – I want to understand this... how's it? Hybristophilia. To know what I've got to be dealing with, what's going on?"

Simmons smiled. "I think that's very smart. Understanding the psychology of it, of yourself, will be a major step in coping with the paraphilia. I can direct you to some research and texts that might help."

The inmate looked at the doctor, steel brimming in his eyes. "Yes," he begged, his voice steady. "Tell me it all, exactly. I have to know."

By the end of the session, a strange energy had settled on Jason, a renewed determination to explore the macabre world of hybristophilia and its potential implications for him.

He thought that understanding was power: that one day, if he could isolate the forces at work, he might finally regain control of his narrative, his destiny.

So, taking a deep breath and nodding to Dr Simmons, he walked out of his doctor's study and into his future, into whatever truths about himself remained to be discovered.

For the days after his session, he was beset with a new desire: to 'study the hell out of hybristophilia'. He plunged into the limited science of this paraphilia, reading every psychology book and article he could find, his eyes burning in the flickering light of a cell block as he devoured blandly academic pages.

The abundance of information initially overwhelmed him, a chaotic blend of theories and case studies. But gradually, patterns emerged, connecting the dots of his past.

He delved into the complexities of hybristophilia, learning about its various forms and the underlying psychological factors. The more he read, the more he saw unsettling parallels to his life.

But it was the case studies that bothered him the most, the stories of real people who had allowed a sexual attraction to a very dark side of humanity to take over their lives. There was the woman who fell for a serial murderer. There was the man who aided his wife's escape from prison. Then, all the others threw away their families, their careers, and even their identity in the name of a deviant S–O–B.

Reading about obsession and despair, he was struck by the strong resemblance the stories bore to his own: they reminded him of the letters that Jamal and Emma had sent him, how excited they had made him at first, and then how horrified. Were they hybristophiles? Or were they more than that? Did their admiration for him reflect some deeper pathology, something beyond the mere obsession with delinquency that might drive them, too, to seek out a killer?

As he read, the question grew: 'If you are a willing participant in a psychic game that is a matter of life and death, are you still a victim? Is there a role for chance and innocence? Or is some part of you nonetheless drawn to this? Can you unconsciously sense what the other person reads in you without knowing yourself? Maybe.'

He thought about the night his father had died: the rage, the drink in his veins, the sound of splintering bone against wood. At the time, it had felt like catharsis, a final desperate blow to a life spent in chains. But now, in daylight, Jason wondered if there wasn't something more to it than that.

Perhaps unconsciously, maliciously, had he all along wished his father dead? Was the murder a kind of wish fulfilment, a means of asserting some mastery over a world that had always seemed to be sabotaging him?

The idea made him queasy, but he couldn't shake it. The more he read about hybristophilia, the more signs of it he detected in himself, in his twisted emotional wiring, in his shadowy nooks of anger and resentment and in the roots of insanity that sprouted in his mind.

After the fans, the faceless millions who had turned him into a folk hero, a criminal, a rebel against the machine. he had always revelled in their support and attraction to his radical ways. Now, he realised, he was seeing them in a new light.

Or were they admirers or grave robbers who fed off his infamy, at once starving and contributing to his body politics, flaying him in their imaginations and discourse as human or beast? Was he a subject or an object?

He spent more and more time with these questions. The more he spent with them, the more it felt like he was slowly slipping over a precipice, that somehow, he was losing his link with reality, that the boundaries between fact and truth, good and evil, were turning fuzzy. He no longer knew where he found himself.

But even as the seeds of doubt and the visions of the adversary came encroaching on his mind, he realised he couldn't turn back, stop digging, searching because somewhere within the sinuous grimoire of hybristophilia and its entanglements, he knew that his own story, his plant pseudoscience, was still somehow embedded. He knew that, somewhere within those many volumes, his story could offer him, once again, a key.

And so he'd turn the page, feeling lonely and miserable, and go on reading, straining his eyes from one page to the next, down the mind's staircase, not knowing where he was going or what would happen.

Even if it pulled him to places, he hadn't wanted to go to the shadows of his soul and the knots of anger, grief and terror that had brought him to the brink of the abyss, even if it made him lose himself.

## 19. Emma and Jamal

The more significant the rise of Jason's 'hero' status became, the more prominent Emma's campaign, the more Jason's own carefully worded letters, and the more intensely consumed Jamal grew with a sense that all this was quickly slipping from his fingertips. He had been following Jason from the outset. He had indeed felt for the first time in his life a kind of elation, a magnificence, a deep connectedness with the young man whose experiences were somewhat reminiscent of his own, and not least perhaps because they were persistently crystallised through his letters and on Emma's social media feeds.

But the more time passed, the more disconcertingly dubious Jamal became that Jason's replies to his letters, already sporadic, were all too much for him to bear an increasing dissipation from his life.

'If this is love,' he thought, 'then I have to meet the man I love. I have to visit him in prison, and I have to face the real world and see whether what I felt with Jason is love or whether it is all in my mind.'

He knew he had to break free from his family's expectations and principles. He felt that even if it was a long time he had no contact with them, he was still entangled in their bigot principles. At the same time, the sadness and disappointment he felt for his sexual identity scared him. He remained intensely devoted to his faith for many years – but the idea that he was gay was haunting. Ultimately, he decided to go and meet Jason. This time, he was determined to stand by him. It was a decision that could have changed his life.

He shivered as he filled out the application, knowing he had to weave words that would convince the warden, knowing the future was riding on a few lines of piss, but he did it anyway. He would get his chance. He would look into Jason's eyes and hear his voice. He would feel whole. He smiled tightly, already inside his fantasy, knowing it would shift his life, although the odds seemed stacked against him. 'They're pretty strict about visits at this place.' But deep down, he had to believe. He had to try.

He checked the mail compulsively and didn't have to wait days for a reply. He stiffened every time some noise announced the arrival of yet another e-mail. The one that eventually arrived didn't contain the news he had been praying for. The guards had denied his request for a visit with Jason: his correspondence said that it was due to security reasons and because his case had become high-profile.

Then, as if the world had sucker-punched Jamal in the solar plexus, deflating his lung upon lung completely, it snatched that lingering possibility away from him. He had been so close. Agonisingly close.

For some time, he did nothing but sit in his room, gawping at his walls and trying to understand the swirl of feelings in his head. Angry, betrayed, that the Universe was against him, that it was determined to keep him from the one thing that meant the most to him.

But even as the agony and anger took its toll, even as it threatened to bring him to his knees, he sensed he wouldn't be himself if he didn't continue to hope, to search for some way to connect that he couldn't be anything else within his own heart and conscience. And again, with even greater intensity, he threw himself into the search that had rapidly become his obsession, pouring over everything he could find about Jason and his case.

He began marching and picketing with Emma's swelling troupe of supporters, standing at the front with a hand-written placard professing his devotion and love for Jason across the country. He sent letters to policymakers and reporters asking them to re-examine the injustices of Jason's case and the *corrupt system* putting him in prison.

And all the while, he was once not thinking of Jason, never once not imagining the day when they would be together, when nobody else would ever hurt him again –whatever that *not ever* might mean.

It was a dangerous infatuation, already occupying most of his waking hours... But every fibre in his brand new being screamed: 'Who cares? Who cares about anything but the connection you've been searching for all your life?'

Then he kept going, propelled by a power he did not fully comprehend but that he knew, at his very bones, was the means of his redemption. He would reach Jason somehow, by some means; he would defy death itself, if need be, whatever stood in his way.

Even at the cost of everything else – even at the expense of self-annihilation. For there is nothing more. There is only the swim towards that radiant light and the ultimate touch.

His room, littered with the detritus of his obsession: the letters, the newspaper cuttings, the scrolling ticker tape of online celebrity worship – filled with a grim determination. He was not to be denied; no one could stop him, and no fate destined him for anything but a winner.

And if the world tried to stop him, if oppression and injustice wanted to keep him from his rightful place by Jason's side?

And then he'd burn everything down, rend the very powers that be until nothing was left but the two of them and the blood they shared.

By the end, it was just Jason who counted. He would never let a man, woman, or anything else come between him and his love again.

## *20. Michael Jones*

Michael Jones had grown into a lifelong friend of the Whites from his own, similarly rough East End boyhood. Though he and Harry had come from respectably poor backgrounds in that tough neighbourhood, Michael had defied the odds – he put himself through law school before moving to Brussels for several years to practise with a firm there.

This is how Michael met and married his wife. This friendly, cultured Belgian woman persuaded him to see beyond the parochialism of his childhood world. Even after they eventually moved back to live in London's East End, the Whites remained at the centre of his world, a source of regular visits, outings, and celebrations.

Although the paths of these lifelong friends had gone in radically different directions, with Harry mired in a series of manual labour jobs, Michael respected an old friend and his family. But little signals over time – furtive glances, abrupt subject changes, and, most tellingly, the rare but unmistakable bruises and injuries that he saw on Germaine's body – confirmed that not all was well in the White household.

Though the sharp creases in his well-tailored suit could have belonged to any stuffy barrister, Michael's open countenance and ease of movement hinted at a more streetwise demeanour moulded by years of navigating the East End's rough streets. His cropped, greying hair and deep-set eyes provided glimpses of the hard-nosed kid from the poor side of the tracks. At the same time, the authoritative jut of his jawline signalled the self-assured professional he had become.

When he attempted to broach the topic of the apparent evidence of abuse, Germaine put forth perfunctory, disdainful explanations about being uncoordinated and accident-prone. On the other hand, unattractive, intimidating Harry seemed to enjoy witnessing his wife's diversion. When the two of them stared back at him, Michael saw aggression that made it clear when he was to cross the line. His gut may have told him something more was happening, but his absence of tangible proof stopped him from further pursuing the matter.

So, that day, after Harry's provocation by Jason, Germaine called him in a panic, and he abandoned his bed and drove a few miles from his East London home to Germaine's house. He heard his friend explain over hysterical sobs the verbal standoff that had developed. Moving decisively into combat mode, Jason had pushed

Harry back, and then the crack as the elderly man's head hit the corner of a table.

To Michael's ears, schooled in the realm of law, Germaine's narrative made what was the worst possible case for self-defence — domestic escalation spilling over into accidental homicide; it was a story that depicted every detail and motive for perfect clarity, leaving no obvious exaggeration, omission or inconsistency to trigger a red light in the investigators' minds. And anyway, he had two children to look after, whose needs could sometimes provoke tensions that built, like pressure cookers, between husband, kids and wife until one or other snapped, without knowing exactly how mortal the loss of temper might be.

Promising Germaine that he'd do his best to see that Jason got a fair hearing and maybe even a complete acquittal, he got right down to business. He met with Jason, still in a dazed state. He repeated the message about telling it like it happened. On the strength of Germaine's testimony, he reported he was at least hopeful he could get the charges against her son reduced from murder to a lesser count of manslaughter, at worst.

But none of his thoroughness and eloquent defence at trial could trump the scale of damning evidence: following that terrible blow to the head, the trajectory of Jason's flight after the fact allowed the prosecution to construct a credible scenario for premeditated violent intent flowing from darker impulses. At the trial, the jury found the boy guilty of manslaughter, and he was incarcerated for many years by the time he was still very young.

Only after the verdict did harsh truths emerge in a late-night sob by hearer-of-last-words Germaine: "Yes, that evening... in the last moment... when Harry was no longer moving, then you... did something to him... you wanted to spare you all that suffering... Did

I hear correctly what you have just told me, ol' lady? Or is there anything to what I heard? Answer clearly: "My friend, I swear to you that when the fighting stopped, and Harry was still, I killed him because I didn't want him to continue to trouble us. You will see, it was for our good... and so that he would never again bother me or my children."

This speech was decisive: it provided evidence of a voluntary act. It eliminated self-defence as a justification for the killing.

The horrific depravity of Germaine's ruse induced in him a concomitant retrospective understanding of the apparent contradiction of that oddly placid composure she'd displayed upon those initial retellings. Michael was unable to deny the extenuating circumstances of the battering that his friend's wife had suffered. Nor could he so readily shrug off the nurturing protectiveness, the desperation for survival – however warped – that had to have spawned those acts.

Rather than walk away, Michael also chose to remain with the White family, even if his function was now a shade of grey. He shifted his 'official' efforts on behalf of Jason into carefully drafting appeals and anticipating strategies that could one day overturn his godson's conviction if new evidence or permissible testimony from Germaine ever provided an avenue for exoneration. It is a question of the moral texture of one's conscience. Deciding what you can live with.

And so he waited, planning and hoping that day Germaine would save her son from the infamy he was accused of and cleanse her consciousness after she took responsibility for the deeds.

## 21. *A tough decision*

The heavy metal door to his six times four-metre visitation booth had just rattled open. Jason was torn out of reverie, his head snapping up to see his lawyer and godfather enter through that door. "You got a still beating heart, boy?" chuckled Michael, his eyes searching for some change in Jason's expression since he'd last visited him two months before. "You're becoming a legend out there," he continued, half smiling. "I need you to stop rocking, though..." referring to the Social Media success his case was enjoying.

No reaction from Jason.

"Jason," Michael questioned, his voice soft but with a hint of concern lingering at the edges. "You, okay?"

Jason shrugged, his eyes dropping to the floor – as though he might get dirt on them. "What you're expecting," he replied. "As well as can be expected. What's up?"

Michael sat opposite Jason, his briefcase on the table between them. His gaze travelled to Jason's face. "I wanted to just talk about this idea of appealing. I guess... I want you to make a decision. You and I have talked about whether you think it's possible. But we need to decide."

The young man felt dizzy; his chest tightened in a swoon. He felt subject to forces far more significant than himself, and he didn't know how he would keep it all together. The thought of an appeal had weighed on him for months. He hadn't consciously considered his mother's confession; he had harboured a desperate wish for the death sentence.

"I don't know," he confirmed almost in a whisper. "I just.... I don't know how I'm going to do it."

"Boy," Michael interjected, leaning forward, his body tense, "I know it's a lot to ask, and I wouldn't go over your head and ask for an appeal if it wasn't important. You have to look to your future and the life you want to build for yourself, and an appeal could be your possibility to start over and leave all this stuff behind."

Jason shook his head, and his eyes burned with tears he was reluctant to let fall. "But my mum? What she did... how can I forgive her for that? I have thought about it, and the answer I came up with is that I am thinking of Anita. And this wipes off any chance I can see her taking my place in this seat."

Weighing his decision, the lawyer sighed. "I know it's tough. I know it's hard. I know your mother decided long ago that she would do things a certain way, and she will have to live the rest of her life with her decisions," sighing and moving back on his chair, combing his hipster hair with both hands. "But you have to learn to be proactive. You have to learn to be tough. You have to make decisions for yourselves. You can't just let your mother control you and fuel your sense of guilt."

Jason's anger flared up like a matchstick. "And what about Anita? What are we going to do about my sister? How can you walk away from her and leave her to deal with what our mother did? How do you think losing the other parent would impact her? She's happy my Dad died. She writes and tells me that Mum and she are happy. I am the only piece missing to make their happiness complete. How can I do that?"

Michael considered this for a minute. "You know your sister is worried about you," he murmured. "But you're not your mother. You didn't make her do what she did and won't make her pay for it by forgoing your future."

Jason felt a flood of weariness wash over him, the decision bearing down on him like an oncoming tide. He knew his lawyer was right, somewhere deep down. He couldn't let his mother choose his life for him; he had to think about his future and the kind of life he'd like.

However, turning his back on his family, on Anita left to cope alone in the aftermath of their mother's extreme act of hate... was itself a violation, a betrayal of the unspoken, unspeakable ties that had bound them together through years of violence and hardship.

"I don't know if I can," he finally mouthed. "I don't know if I'm tough enough to bear the consequences."

Michael laid a floppy, lumpy hand across the top of Jason's arm. "You're strong, mate." His voice was even and steady. "Then you know. Whatever you decide. I shall be here for you."

For some reason, Jason suddenly felt grateful.

"Thank you," he sighed, his voice thick with emotion. "Thank you for everything."

His godfather smiled. "Don't thank me, boy. That's what I get paid for." He laughed, knowing that Jason knew nobody was paying for his services. He stared directly at him. "That's my calling. It's my honour to be there by your side. You have proven to be a better man than both your parents despite being raised by them. You are the proof that genetics can fuck itself when it comes to morality and honour."

Sitting together, each lost in their thoughts, Jason realised there wasn't an easy way out without hurting someone. It wasn't going to be straightforward.

But he also knew that he was not alone. He had people who believed in him and would stand up for him, even for the wrong reason.

"I want to do it," he finally resolved, his voice even and firm. "I want to appeal."

Michael nodded, a smile of pride and respect lighting the eyes. "Then that's what we'll do," he rushed with an expression of satisfaction printed on his face. "Jason? We'll make a team," he whispered, trying to sound confident. "We'll fight this war. And we'll win it."

As the two men shook hands, their palms gently squeezing, muscles flexing, reminding them that lifting heavy things would be needed to force the full depth of this particular rut, Jason found himself struck suddenly by the actual possibility of freedom, the daunting idea that there was a way out of this world he had been living for the last three years. A world made of lies to others and himself. The hero would have fought with every atom to get out. He was innocent. He knew it.

What mattered soon was only truth and the freedom freed by truth, however painful and challenging it may be.

And he was ready to die to make that challenge stick – and to claim that truth and freedom for himself.

In the days after he met Michael, he felt the presence of a new imperative. His work on hybristophilia and his growing awareness of psychological forces penetrated his own past: "My approach was one of a more active re-examination and review ... I was digging quite deeply into the past." He would have said later.

At first, they came only gradually, as flickering insights at the periphery of his attention. He began to trace lines connecting his adult behaviour to his childhood experiences of being systematically abused and neglected by his father. He was amazed at how the human brain can hide, remove, or refuse to see the truth when love and fear are involved and self-protection is needed.

He recalled the dread and uncertainty, that deep sense of inadequacy, of never being good enough, of never being what his father felt he should be. And he understood how those feelings had haunted him throughout his still-young life. He saw how they continued to drive him – to crave the approval and validation of others, sometimes to the extent of subordinating his own needs to obtain it.

However, as he rummaged through his past, he became more persistent. As he began to narrate his life events through his burgeoning self-analysis, his conclusions became increasingly bizarre and overwrought. Everything—even his crime—could be traced back to psychological theories he had been reading about.

The letters fueled a growing obsession with hybristophilia. He saw its dark patterns reflected in his own life: his infatuation with Emma, his connection with Jamal, even the act that had landed him in prison. Had he subconsciously craved his father's death, a twisted act of defiance against a lifetime of oppression? His mother's silence, her complicity, only deepened the sense of worthlessness that gnawed at him. Was he truly unlovable, undeserving of happiness?

Because his self-analysis turned upon itself, more and more impoverished and distorted, the longer he did it, the more alienated he became, more and more the slave of his inner narrative. Hour after hour alone in his cell, he would read through his old journals, letters, and anything he could find, combing endlessly for clues and hidden meanings that were glaringly obvious.

He refused to meet Dr Simmons as the seances were becoming too painful to bear.

He was eventually convinced that everything in his life was 'connected', that it was all part of a conspiracy to keep him imprisoned, weakened and subdued.

Jason's behaviour became more and more erratic, sometimes lashing out at cowering guards and inmates, insisting that they were all part of a non-identifiable conspiracy against him, sometimes pacing for hours and hours, convinced that his food was being spiked, or that he was being poisoned at night through chemicals in the mattress, that demons were tormenting him.

Yet he would continue to embrace his new persona: the heroic champion of integrity and morality, the man fated to 'break free' the filthy lie that had so long jailed him.

Still, as his mind assured him everything was fine, a tiny part of him intuitively told him the opposite. 'Isn't this me losing myself? The very thing I used to see myself free of, my intelligence, my insight, my ability to navigate the world with my mind, is now driving me crazy.'

And in his in-between moments of sanity, as he recalled them, he would experience a hopeless grimness in realising that he was locked within the walls of his mind, his damned pathology.

It was an awareness that threatened to bring him down and rupture the precarious sense of self he'd constructed through years of struggle. But it was also an awareness that, if he were brave enough, could lead to redemption.

For this was the only way he would escape the labyrinth of his psyche, the cycle of repeating the same mistakes; the way Jason would move forward, would re-join the world (his world, not one of the illusions) and take back control of his life, no matter how painful the truth might have been, no matter how hopeless and dark his existence had once appeared. For him, the truth was the way forward. To shed the shadows, to wash clean the dirty windows (the layers of distortion and self-deception that had thickened over time), and to finally see himself and his life as they were. Even at the expense of self-obliteration. Even if it meant walking through the most dreadful and twisted aspects of his psyche.

But still, the truth mattered. In the end, truth mattered. That was all. And he wasn't about to rest until he had found it himself.

In the days after his decision to appeal, he was on a rollercoaster of activity: he and Michael Jones hunted down witnesses, dug for evidence, dramatised and rallied defences.

For hours, Jason pored over case files with the lawyer in those rooms, his eyes burning from reading through the fine print as his mind raced. This was his shot, his only shot, to appeal the terrible travesty of justice that had cost him his freedom.

Michael outlined the strategy at their meetings, his voice ringing with authority but laced with fear: "We need to undermine the prosecution's story," he resolved. "Prove that what you did that night wasn't motivated, that you never even wanted to kill your father."

Jason nodded, his mouth set. "I'll go back to the stand – I'll take this son of a bitch to trial again – and tell them the story the way it is this time."

That sense of hope grew again as their appeal approached its court date. He also started to imagine a life outside these prison walls, fresh with possibility.

Still, having allowed himself the faintest glimmer of hope, he remained wary, able to steel himself for the disappointment that the system could still deliver him, that dreams could still shatter.

What would his mother's reaction be? Would she admit her deeds? Would she be believed or accused of taking the blame for freeing her child? What would Anita think about the whole thing? Will she hate him for the price her mum will pay to save him?

## 22. The Accident

And then, one day, on a bright afternoon, a guard walked up to him as he was being taken back from the prison library and told him: "We have some bad news, White."

"White," the guard bellowed. "You need to go with me. Someone's got some bad news for you."

His heart sank, his mind jumping to worst-case scenarios. Something with Anita? Michael? A litany of questions thundered through his head as he was taken to the warden's office.

The warden met Jason's stare. He stared back up at him, looking at him in the eyes for the first time and displaying an expression that Jason couldn't precisely identify – pity, maybe, or regret?

"I'm afraid I have some bad news, son," announced the warden, astonishingly gentle. "It's your mother..."

Then the air rushed out of Jason's lungs, his body involuntarily tensed. He didn't know he loved her so much. The very idea of losing his mother was like a physical blow.

"She was killed in an accident this afternoon. She was crossing the road on the Chiswick roundabout, and this drunk driver ran a red light and hit her. I'm so sorry she didn't make it."

The words swirled around and lodged in Jason's head, the grief and disbelief pounding him into submission, pounding back 'my mother': the agent of his existence, 'my mother?' the protectress and enemy – she was dead.

It was Jason's culmination. His world had collapsed. He had the appeal, the opportunity for a fresh start, and then... this enormity.

With his head in his hands, his face streaked with tears, the warden put a hand on his shoulder and provided whatever comfort he could. The young man scarcely heard a word as images enveloped him amid the previously familiar and loving people – his mother singing as she tucked him into bed, her arms wrapping around him as his father berated him.

And then something in him broke. He realised what she had done: she had killed his freedom, had sentenced him to this squalid life in prison for her. She had betrayed him. Love and betrayal: a knot that tied her life and his together; a knot that for him remained forever unbroken, even after death.

Now, in the wake of Germaine's death, the appeal seemed to be slipping away without purpose. How could Jason show that he had not killed his Dad when no one had testified to the facts when no one had taped her confession?

The entire world collapsed around him. He cursed himself for not having spoken earlier. His mum, the reason why she was in prison and the only one who could have gotten him out, was dead. A drunkard had taken away from him the last hope to be free—bloody alcohol. Again, alcohol had shuttered his life.

Days passed, and Jason refused to see or talk to anyone. He was granted a special permit to attend Germaine's funeral, but he declined. He didn't feel like celebrating the life of the woman who betrayed him. He would not have the guts to face Anita or anyone else. He didn't want to put on a show if he had gone ballistic. He couldn't. He could not be there.

Michael tried to coax him and light the fire again in that blackened core. "We still have a case to make, man." He paused. "Your mother's death doesn't change the facts of the matter."

But Jason was untethered, no longer bound by his belief in what he had been driven to do. His mother's death had severed his last tie to the truth – and, with it, to reality.

And as the days turned into weeks, he wrestled with the grief, then began to doubt, his conviction in the appeal eroding by the hour. He was haunted by his memory of his sweet and despondent mother, each an illustration of the qualities she embodied.

Sometimes, he felt that he may have deserved it, that he had angered the gods and was being punished; they had finally come to collect on the debt and had hoisted him up here, imprisoned for a reason. Maybe they were keeping him confined not only in these walls but also in his mind.

Still, that little bit of hope never entirely went away. In the back of his head, that same whisper crept in. He would not succumb to despair or let what had happened destroy him. Not after all he'd been through.

And so, strengthening himself through his grief, he prepared for the battle ahead. He would end the war with the truth, knitting a path between his mother's love and neglect as he claimed both sides of his ancestral inheritance.

As the day of the appeal hearing approached, he stood before the mirror in his cell, reflecting on all he had lost and what he still might win.

"I'll never disappoint you like you did with me, Mum. But, the truth should be known." "OK," she murmured, not very encouragingly. "Somehow. Now, what next?" He squeezed her shoulder. "All right. Well, I'd better get back to work." He reassured quietly, "One way or the other, the truth will be known."

And with that, he took a last look back and walked off into the future, his feet on the ground and his heart steady.

Then he woke up, drenched in sweat.

Jason's hands shook as he scanned the newspaper, his eyes locking on the headline that seemed to shout from the page:

*Woman Linked to High-Profile Manslaughter Case Killed in Tragedy.*

He had asked the warden for the papers to understand what happened to his mum. But nothing could have prepared him for the sucker punch that was the sight of Mom's name in print. Her death was reduced to a mere footnote in the tragedy around which the entire story had revolved.

When he read over the details of the accident – drunk driver... hit in a crosswalk... the horrendous cries of twisting steel – Jason's gut lurched in the nauseating churn of grief and disbelief. She had been ripped away in an instant of boneheaded violence.

It offered his past, the house of cards that tragedy made of his family, how his father died that night and how their lives could never be the same. Jason could hear their voices in the news, even if they had not watched TV in three years. He imagined them full of innuendo, all salacious talk and veiled judgment: the body found in his bedroom, the shock of Jason's conviction, his mother's duplicity unrevealed.

This article described the latest twist in the ongoing saga of his sentence and the long-awaited appeal. *Germaine White is dead by his son's hand*, the passage read, *and without her testimony, his defence may fall apart. Germaine White was an accessory victim of her son, Jason.*

He crumpled the newspaper in his hands, the paper crackling under the pressure, and felt the walls shrinking in on him. The hope gripped him through the past few months was slipping away.

He was lost, unable to cling to the frail rope that had evoked his spirit during his very worst years inside. The truth that he held fast to, like a bleeding finger and a splintered branch above the face of a drowning man, was gone. He was back in his loneliness and under the control of a system that had forsaken him once before.

What he read at once seemed to dissolve in the chaotic combination of the accident narrative and the account of his own disgraceful past until each had become a single blend of agony and remorse. He felt himself being pressed by that emotion's force and gravity to the depths of the abyss.

His eyes filled with tears, and he blinked them away, angered by its near-limitless strength, which made him susceptible to its drowning pull. He could not have come this far and endured this much just to be beaten down now in this fashion.

Still, as much as he resolved to move forward, he couldn't help but question whether the cosmos itself was against him, that he had been judged unworthy of forgiveness and was to be doomed to a life of regret, lost perpetually in the multitude of his sins.

As he folded the newspaper and laid it aside, he felt the mantle of darkness descend upon him, the manifestation of a crushing weight of an inevitable destiny bearing down upon his heart. The road before him had seemed to bristle with a scarcely perceptible hope. Now, it stretched before him in looming gloom.

But a sliver of defiance still sparked in him, a refusal to allow the blackness to claim him in full. He would go on: one step and then another. Somewhere in those steps, the Truth that remained forever true – somewhere under the rubble of his wrecked life – would come spilling out to save him.

## 23. *Anita*

It was stifling in the visitation room, the air heavy with anxiety and unsaid words. Jason drummed his fingers anxiously on the table while waiting for his sister to arrive. It had been three years since he had seen Anita, and now, thrust by his mother's recent death into an uncomfortable and unavoidable re-grouping, his sickly brew of dread and impulse to please was on full display.

When the thick door finally groaned open, Jason started to draw a sharp breath of air when Anita shuffled in, her shoulders rounded, her eyes red and swollen. She looked smaller somehow, her weight and sorrow taking a toll on her. Jason's heart ached at the sight. She was a woman now, soon to be eighteen, but she was no longer the girl he used to tease for "the skinny legs and lack of breasts." She used to get upset and pay him back with insults. But they loved each other and knew that none meant terrible. Jason and Annie, as he used to call Anita, were partners in crime. They would be there for each other and love each other fondly.

Today, a woman entered that room. She was beautiful, stunning. Jason was terrified. He didn't know whether this woman was his little Annie or someone else who had taken over her body.

They were both silent momentarily, the gulf between them as solid and unbreachable as any ocean. Then the young woman smiled—or tried to. Her lips quivered with the effort.

"Hey, big brother," she uttered, her voice barely above a whisper.

He swallowed hard, his smile feeling more like a grimace. "Hey, sis."

Anita moved gradually to a chair on the opposite side of him, struggling to focus as if trying to see through a thick haze. He saw the dark circles under his sister's eyes and the sunkenness of her cheeks; these were signs of her insomnia, he thought, clues to grief burrowing deep into her tissues.

"How are you?" he asked. It seemed like a ludicrous question, almost an insult, as he knew how much she had suffered.

"I'm surviving," was the reply. Anita's eyes looking down at her hands clasped on the table. The heavy sorrow in her voice betrayed her previous quiet confidence. "Some days are better than others."

Jason nodded. He knew how grief could come and go, dominate, then fade to a dull ache. Anita muffled something. He didn't hear her; he was lost in his thoughts. She waved her hand in front of him to draw his attention.

"I got hired," she announced without any enthusiasm. "There. I start next week. Not glamorous, waitressing. A café. But it's something to do, you know? Something so I don't feel sorry for myself all day."

Envy, a trace of guilt – that's how he often saw his confinement. He had many things to do, and Anita gradually reclaimed her life. Meanwhile, he was still fenced in, doomed to eternal waiting.

"That's great, Anita." And he meant it. "I'm proud of you that this hasn't got the better of you."

She looked at him and gave him a small, tight, grateful smile. But it was soon gone, and her face fell again. "No, it's not easy," she made clear. "I wake up every day, and for a split second, I think she's still here. Then I remember the pain, and it hits me again like a punch in the stomach."

He nodded. "I know," he replied. "I know." The ache came back into his throat. He swallowed hard. He knew. "You always thought she was perfect, didn't you?" She asked.

He nodded.

They slumped again into silence, each caught up in their respective interior spaces, each lost in their respective pasts. Jason studied his sister's face, trying to detect hints of the laughing girl he had once known, the girl he had grown up with.

But that girl was dead, killed off by the wreckage of their destroyed family and replaced by a woman who'd seen and suffered far too much, far too soon.

The air had become thick in its silence, and he finally did the talking.

"Anita, there's something I need to tell you..."

Tension was rife. She stopped him.

"Why, Jase? Why didn't you come to Mum's funeral?"

He gulped. "I couldn't, sis, not after that. What she ..."

She furrowed her brow. She was confused and perhaps a bit angry. "What? What do you mean? Mum died in an accident. She didn't do anything. She just loved us."

He shook his head, and then his eyes met his sister's, beseeching her to comprehend.

"What Mum said is not right – she killed Dad – she told me so."

The words marked their position, reality but an arm's length away.

"You're lying. You're lying because you are scared shitless that the truth will come out, and people will see that you murdered Dad. You're scared shitless that people will realise it's you who purposely killed Dad and that it was you who tore this family to shit."

Jason flinched as if a blow had been struck at his heart. "Anita, please believe me. I wouldn't lie about something like this. Mum told me, she told me, that she'd finished Dad off after I pushed him. She let me take the rap to protect you."

His sister shook her head and began to weep. "Stop it! Just stop! Mum would never have done that. She loved us, loved Dad, even when he could be hard work. You're just trying to excuse yourself. I would appreciate it if you would tell me what you probably tell yourself. You did what you had to do."

He could feel his tears prickling his eyes. "Annie, I'm swearin' to you, I'm bein' true. Mum had to do it to keep you safe. She thought I would be acquitted... I had a better chance of gettin' off in the trials. Of gettin' out, maybe."

Her look turned cold, and her lips puckered into a thin line. "Save your bullshit for someone who gives a crap, Jason, you are dead to me. Mum deserved better than what you did to her, even in death."

With this, she whirled and stomped out the door, creating gunshot sounds with her footfalls in the uncomfortable quiet she'd left behind. Jason looked up at her, and his heart shattered, his mind an ocean of grief and his soul in wide-open agony.

Once again, he found himself in the depths of solitude, imprisoned by his own truth – which exacted a heavy toll on his family, his freedom, and now, even his sister's love.

For a moment, he was overwhelmed by the sheer weight of his existence, a burden he could not lift. At this moment, he questioned himself, 'I've fought for the truth – but at what cost? Is the price of my honesty ... too steep? ... too merciless?'

Choking back a sob, he buried his face in his hands. He shamefully shook with silent grief, the appeal, the right to be cleared of this dreadful accusation, seeming trivial in the face of such loss.

But even now, even while near despair, a spark of defiance remained. It was not enough that they conquer, that they stand in triumph upon the wreckage of all he held dear: not here, not now, not ever. From this, he would not yield; it was the one thing he had left, and he would take his stand here, whatever the cost, the darkness, whatever the end.

With his head up, now fiery-eyed, he knew the road ahead would be rough, and he'd be banged and bruised on the way, but, this time, he'd walk it, one step at a time, until either he died or found the redemption he sought.

## 24. Jamal and Emma

With the publicity came a reckoning that Jamal had long dreaded. His vocal support for Jason and his explicit professions of affection had not gone unnoticed. The Muslim community that he had valued so much was not thrilled about his honesty.

Whispers told one to another with no shortage of condemnation and thinly veiled disgust. "He's an abomination," an elder hissed, the words as sharp as a dagger through Jamal's heart. "A stain on our faith, a blemish on our traditions."

The backlash was furious and brutal. "If I were to show up at my uncle's house now, they wouldn't want me to be part of the wedding. The people I spoke to don't want me to be part of their life, sit, or eat with them. It's been a backlash. People are sending me disgusting messages, saying, *You're a faggot, you deserve to die, you ruined my family.*" He was ostracised.

Still, he stuck to his ideals—his love for Jason was a flame to light his way—and threw himself into the international audiences who had taken up their cause, who provided reassurance that many voices can make it easier to hear your own.

"People just don't get it," he confided to a fellow fan late one night on video chat. "They can't get past their narrow-mindedness to appreciate the wholesome difference Jason and I make together."

His conviction hardened as the trial neared: 'I will make him love me. I will have complete happiness.' He stared at Jason's photo, his reflection a stranger. 'But it's still me,' he thought desperately. 'It's still me.'

At the same time, Emma was facing her own demons. Rumours about her own life began to spread – extraordinarily dark tales – a backstory that not only spoke to how early she had been institutionalised but also could be used to discredit her.

"You ever hear about her childhood?" one classmate to another, tone dripping with schadenfreude. "Apparently, her father was a total arsehole, you know, she beat her up and everything. Classic tale. You know what I mean."

What eventually began to emerge – like so often happens with her – was the truth creeping through the cracks of her 'dossier', revealing that here was a girl fixated on Jason as a way of masking a lifetime of trauma and unprocessed pain.

Nevertheless, even as the murmurs mounted, she remained resolved. She dismissed the chatter as the intrigues of little minds. She devoted her energy to the cause she had regarded as her life's purpose.

"They can talk," her voice rising, on a Facebook Live video broadcast. "But they can't talk about that connection I have to Jason, that love, that feeling, that spirit that we have, that we come from the same place, that we both saw the dark and made it out to the other side."

Meanwhile, her commitment to Jason increased as the trial approached. She wanted to see him vindicated, to see him beat the system that had hurt him so grievously—that much-needed victory, the one she and Jason believed would free them both from the demons that had plagued them for too long.

And so, with the world watching and waiting, Jamal and Emma stood their ground, each marching to their own drummer while also marching together – each bonded to Jason – fighting their legal and soul battles not just in court but also for their identities and the social signifiers of what being male or female is.

After all, their stories were not just a backdrop and not just a sidebar to the Jason story: they were stories, too, part of a moment in time when a trial had captured the attention of a nation. And as they prepared themselves for what was to come, for whatever change would ensue, they knew that, for good or for bad, their lives would never be the same due to the Jason White storm that blew through them. They were already seeing the effects of their fixation on someone they thought was a murderer and to which they were both morbidly attracted.

In the months, as his appeal inched its way through the machinery that would decide Jason's fate, his connections with the outside world grew thinner still. The threads of reality he clung to were fewer and weaker as the vortex of the case spun faster around and around. But things were not getting bleaker. His mailbox was filled with letters that continued to come in through the prison machine from people with whom he exchanged some correspondence in those years in jail—those who pledged to stand by him.

For Emma, his letters were talismans of light in an abyss, and every line promised that her life was joined by his and that their trials proved that the spirit of the human being could never be defeated. She would read every word in every sentence, knowing the act of forming a phrase was testimony to the genius of the man whose talents she had elevated above the mantle of mere mortals.

*My dear Emma,* one began, the sentences blurry in several places where his pen had lingered too long, inking through to the next word. *Your confidence in me is a candle in the darkest night. When I think that this world is crushing me with all its evil and violence, all I have to remember is you and all the friends who stand behind me and turn around to face it all.*

In these words, she found comfort and affirmation. She basked in their power, washing away her natural reservations and hesitations, her melodramatic personal insecurities, as Jason's gratitude poured down like a great waterfall of emotional validation. She would read his letters aloud in her livestreams, her voice shaking with the effort, broadcasting his words for the world to hear, a rallying call to her masses.

"He adores us," she used to exclaim, eyes not yet wet. "He knows that we're his true allies, his true understanding."

And they would respond right back, the voices they would use to reply digital avatars of their adoration and solidarity. To them, Jason's letters were not just important words on an Internet page but also a vindication of the values that made them a group in the first place.

But to Jamal, they were also full of angst, each letter a fresh reminder of the distance separating him from the person at the centre of his universe. He had given everything for Jason – their love was a fire inside him lighting up the sky in the centre of his heart – and yet the response was an empty tribute of letters barely holding any of the deep-felt emotion burning inside him.

*My dear Jamal* ran one such letter, the very style of which smacks of sad irony. *Your suggestions on my behalf fill me with an inexpressible sense of humility, and I shall thank you in person if we ever can meet face to face.*

Jamal would read and re-read, his stomach sinking with each page, acrid bile rising in his throat, the sting of his rejection taking root in his bones. He had unburdened himself and professed his love in the most naked and exposed of terms, and yet Jason's text was superficial in the extreme.

All these months, watching Emma blush with pleasure at the news of another of Jason's ardent missives, all seeing the soft light of that handsome countenance shine from her cheeks, his eyes sting at the prick of such guilty envy, and it seemed it pricked more deeply with each passing day. He gave up everything for this man: his life, his faith, his soul, everything. And it was Emma who was bathed in Jason's light.

The voices of doubt started seeping in, insidious, like a virulent infection spreading inexorably through the body. The ivy of doubt wove itself deftly around his thoughts, constricting his windpipe until he struggled to catch his breath. Jason might not have known what he was saying. Or perhaps he might not have meant it.

Soon enough, the days ran into weeks, and his once unwavering love was brutally eroded by insecurities and hurtful realities that came with being in a position where someone didn't love you back. He would watch Emma on her live stream for hours, his pupils dilated with anguish and his body on fire from unbuffered tears, as he imagined her cuddling up to Jason and describing how much she loved him.

But even so, the seeds of doubt and resentment germinated inside him, Jamal refused to dissociate himself from this terrible cause that was now his *raison d'etre*. He loved Jason with the same desperation that a sunbeam of gamma intensifies to a thousandfold; to snuff it out would be to burn a chapter of himself.

He couldn't stop. He just kept marching and protesting, his feet growing heavier daily; his smile drained itself and turned into a thin shell of its former glowing self. He'd march and yell and call until his throat started to hurt; he'd grow weak, but so far not defeated, holding hope that maybe one day, somehow, Jason would be capable of seeing through those mistaken eyes of his that he was not just another devoted follower, but rather another soul that, through his unfiltered love, he had tied his hefty self to.

Around the world, people waited and watched, their fortunes bound up in Jason's petition; Jamal and Emma walked, virtually hand in hand but helpless, their hearts what separated them as much as what united them.

# Part 4 – The Appeal

## 25. Media Frenzy

With Jason's appeal date approaching, the air almost crackled with tension. Social Media chatter about his case had grown feverish, while devout supporters were sharing a hashtag—*#FreeJason*—in their push to have him freed from prison.

Jamal, the protagonist of this digital storm, had penned a heartfelt letter that bared his soul and proclaimed his love for Jason. His emotional bond with Jason was unbreakable despite the physical separation as if an invisible thread had tethered their souls.

"No, I know he's innocent in my heart," declared Jamal to several fellow protesters just outside the court. "The system failed him the same way it fails so many of us daily."

A chorus of cheers and raised fists answered him, a crowd going wild from his passion like a fire.

"It's not going to stop until he gets out of prison! Start!" shouted into his megaphone, his voice rising above the cacophony of the crowd. "Justice for Jason! Justice for all of us!"

He was NOT short on publicity. His ardent campaigning for Jason led to his base of fans, too; they even created a Twitter hashtag, *#FreeJamal*. The conversation about these men on the internet collided and became one ongoing story.

Emma's obsession with Jason consumed her every waking moment. She poured her heart and soul into the online campaign, her posts growing increasingly fervent, her rhetoric bordering on the fanatical. Her once vibrant social life dwindled as she dedicated every spare moment to the cause, her grades suffering. She saw herself as Jason's saviour, his protector against a world that had wronged him. But beneath the surface, a darker truth lurked: her fascination with his crime, the thrill of the forbidden, fuelled her devotion. At least in her mind, Jason was one of them.

Jamal and Jason were brothers who were fighting against systemic injustice. For months and years, she had spent hours moderating online forums where groups came together to support these causes, whipping up the storm.

The day of appeal was nearing, and the nerves were at an all-time high. The thrill was unmatched. Soon, speculation and conjecture over the case filled social media channels as everyone, from everyday people to experts, shared opinions on who or what was behind it.

*This is an injustice! This would not be properly judged*! one Twitter user ranted. *They locked up the victim while letting a true criminal run free!*

*And who's the criminal that ran free?* Another user would reply.

*He's a danger to society*, posted another. *Being tough on the kids is a sin. That is harsh, I understand, but it does not justify killing one's father.*

Thus, some hailed Jason and Jamal as heroes, and others condemned them as anarchistic zealots. At any rate, one thing remained certain—their stories touched a nerve in the public's eye, and their lyrics became an anthem to many who were shunned by society and oppressed.

Over the next few days, pundits, TV and Radio hosts would have continued to address the Jason White re-trial with opinions as numerous as stars in the sky.

"It's evidence of a complete system failure," declared one expert on the nationally televised news bulletin. "Court heard of the abuse that Jason suffered, but they're only compounding his punishment by having the poor sod still sitting in jail."

"Nonsense!" another guest replied, her face suffused with anger. "He's still guilty of that horrific act, and there is no 'mitigating circumstance' for taking the life of another human being."

The newspapers and online publications were filled with a glut of think pieces, op-eds and articles that dissected the case from every perspective imaginable, fanning flames for an already merciless public conversation.

Jason was also accused of being, inadvertently, the reason why his mother had been killed. For some, it was a further punishment from God for this patricide; for others, Germaine had not been herself since the loss of her husband at the hand of her son. This would have caused her to be distracted when crossing that damn roundabout, well known for being a rough spot for pedestrians and vehicles alike.

Then, the looming question lay at the heart of it all: Would Jason ever get out and be free as he yearned to be? Would the wheels of justice finally churn free, setting him on a path to escaping his prison cage? Or, justice would be served to a difficult and troubled violent young man harbouring hateful thoughts towards a parent?

## 26. Preparing the appeal

Michael Jones held long, anxious meetings with Jason to prepare for the appeal case. A sense of history was building around it. A tide of public noise had flooded into Jason's life, too, and during those nervous months, there was a sense of pressure in the air as the future seemed to become grounded in every word, every stratagem.

Leaning forward in the quiet solitude of the prison visiting room, Jason's face was creased; he was listening.

"We can't use your mother's story in court," Michael mumbled. "Without your mother's testimony, it's hearsay, and they will own it."

Jason nodded in resignation, disappointed but not surprised. Deep in his heart, he knew his mother's confession was not admissible, but he had also stubbornly held onto the hope that it would be his 'get out of jail free' card.

"What do we do, then?" he pleaded. "What do we do if they think I'm a monster?"

Softening, Michael laid his hand across the table on Jason's. "It's all about the facts," he said. "The fact that you've been a model inmate in the past few years, your work toward self-betterment through your therapy and education, we'll have Dr Simmons testify to your progress, to your remorse."

Jason nodded. He was already thinking about how the trial might go wrong. "But what about Anita?" he asked. "She hates me, Michael. You seriously think she's going to say anything good for me?"

The lawyer's jaw hardened, and he let out a deep sigh. "I know. And getting past that is going to be tough. But what choice is there? Can we drop her testimony, Jason? Because if she comes in and confirms the abuse you were both subjected to at your father's hands, the Judges might agree with us."

The young man was sick to his stomach at the prospect of going up against his sister in court, of facing the intimate horror of his childhood out in the open for all to see. But Michael was right. Without Anita, they'd had no case.

"I'll go," Michael reassured him. "I'll talk to her. I'll tell her, and I'll die trying."

Jason nodded, and spectres of pride flashed in Michael's eyes: "That's the way to do it, boy," he concluded.

However, by the end of their meeting, the young man had felt the glimmer of hope ignite.

While outside the prison gates, selfish and sensational public opinion spun like a tornado, demanding retribution.

He would walk into the courtroom, stand in front of the judge and the jury with his chin up, knowing the truth and believing that he would come out of the fires of this crucible a free man, his soul whole and his future to hold.

It was a drastic prospect. Yet it spurred him on. For too long, he'd been bound by the system, self-doubt, and demons of his own making. With the light beginning to shine, he wanted to be a free man, to take hold of that life to which he, quite unjustifiably, felt he had no right.

## 27. *Michael and Germaine*

Michael leaned back in his chair, the weight of Germaine's confession hanging in his dimly lit office. She sat across from him, hands trembling as she recounted the horrific events of that night for the first time.

Her voice trembled as she confessed the truth to Michael. "He was still alive," she whispered, tears streaming down her face. "But I couldn't let him live, not after everything he'd done."

He felt his gut clench as realisation crept in. "Are you saying... Have you finished it? You killed him?"

"Dear God, Germaine," he recoiled, dragging a hand down his face. "Do you realise what you've admitted to? What this means?"

Her expression hardened like brittle stone. "I had to protect my family. You don't know what unending torment it was living under his rule day after day." She began pacing, each step fuelled by decades of pent-up rage and grief. "The bruises, the injuries I've tried to hide from everyone..."

As she spoke, pieces started falling into place for Michael - the suspicious gaps in her stories, the signs of an abusive marriage he had wilfully ignored. "The times you fled the house, went to women's shelters... you filed reports against Harry, didn't you? But then you always recanted and took him back."

A flicker of shame creased her features before the steely facade resumed. "I was terrified of what he might do if I left for good. I had the children and no money, no way out. He had total control."

Michael felt his heart rate quickening as he grasped the devastating implications.

"If this comes out about the abuse reports and shelters, they'll see you as the one who snapped after feeling trapped, not an impulsive crime of passion," he warned her gravely. "They could charge you with first-degree murder."

Her eyes went wide with panic as she clutched at Michael's arm. "Which is why we can't let them know! I only told you out of desperation. If the courts find out I killed him in cold blood like that, they'll..." Her voice cracked as hysteria took hold.

The family friend placed a steadying hand on her shoulder, his legal mind whirring into strategic overdrive. "We have to protect Jason above all else. If they see this as premeditated on your part, he'll be caught in the crossfire, maybe even charged as an accomplice." His tone was grim but resolute. "We have to shape this as an escalating domestic dispute that ended dramatically. You cannot get involved. And Jason should not know what you just told me."

Relief washed over her features as she nodded shakily. "Yes, but you can make it seem I was just another battered wife who snapped..."

"No!" Michael shouted. "You should not be in the picture at all! There's no way that the jury would be lenient towards you. You will be implicated. Anita will end up without a family in the social services system. Think of the implications on her psyche and her future." He asserted. "You were the wife that went to check what had happened. Full Stop! You hear me?"

"Jason snapped and acted defensively in the heat of the moment when the confrontation turned deadly," Michael stated carefully. "Nothing premeditated - one isolated event rather than years of calculated resentment and hatred boiling over."

The weight of his words hung heavy between them. "I know the terrible truth now, my friend. I know the risks and what burying it could cost legally. But to keep that version as our public stance, as the way we present things to protect Jason above all... we can never admit to or discuss the long pattern of abuse that led to this. Are you sure you can keep that buried?"

The murderer stared back at him, a strange combination of defeat and resolve to harden her delicate features. "Harry controlled my life with his fists for far too long. But this is the only thing I can do to wrest some semblance of power from his toxic legacy." Her voice was little more than a hoarse whisper, but it carried the weight of unshakable certainty. "From now on, my sole priority is doing whatever is required to keep my son out of prison, no matter the sacrifice for me."

"Then keep your mouth shut. There are no mentions of the beating, shelters or anything else. Harry had a bad temper, like most fathers of our generation," concluded Michael.

As she steeled herself before his eyes, he realised with a solemn clarity that any semblance of truth had just been interred by the relentless tide of a mother's love. He could only hope that the deceptions they were damning themselves to would be enough to spare Jason from his private hell.

But, after three years in jail, Jason was giving signs of distress, and Michael could no longer be the one to silence the truth. His relationship with the young boy, paying for his mother's deeds, was no longer acceptable to him.

Destiny, though, has a funny way of working things out, and this time, Germaine's death complicates everything. Her death saved his misconduct from jail, and he felt guilty because of his recommendation; a whole family was buried under his lies, but there was no way to free the godson from a crime he did not commit. The only way ahead was to prove that Jason did not represent a danger to society, and he should have found some procedural faults in the first trial to get him freed. But he could not find any.

## 28. *The Appeal*

The courtroom was hushed as Michael rose; his usual dapper appearance was replaced by the melancholy countenance of a man carrying a terrible weight. All eyes were fixed on the now-renowned defence lawyer as he began his opening statement.

"Your honour, the jury, we are gathered here today not to revisit the details of this case," his voice swelled throughout the courtroom. "We are standing in a hall of mirrors reflecting one of the greatest injustices ever perpetrated on a British citizen."

"My client, Jason White, was wrongfully convicted of the charge of voluntary manslaughter three years ago and sentenced to prison where he has sat as an example for a crime he did not voluntarily perpetrate," stated the lawyer.

After the prosecutor's opening statement firmly confirmed the first sentence, Michael's next move was to call an expert witness from Child Protective Services to the stand. The social worker proceeded to lay out a harrowing paper trail - case file after case file detailing the seven separate times Germaine White had reported her husband Harry for domestic violence against herself and her children, only to recant the accusations later each time.

"These records prove a clear pattern of abuse and coerced silence within the White household," the caseworker stated firmly. "On multiple occasions, Mrs. White exhibited signs of physical trauma and would initiate procedures to escape the situation, only to backtrack shortly after, most likely due to threats or financial insecurity."

A grim murmur passed through the rapt courtroom. Michael turned to Jason, who seemed to shrink in on himself, reliving the memories of his tormented childhood.

When it was the prosecution's turn, they played their own trump card—calling Jason's sister Anita to the stand. No longer the timid young girl from before, when she was exempted from testifying during the first trial, her expression was steely as she was sworn in.

"Can you confirm what we heard so far about your father being an abusive man?" asked the prosecutor.

"He was not an easy man. He was always raging but loved us and ensured we never missed out on anything. He could be very caring but had little patience, so he would explode. As far as the violence, I have never witnessed it, and with me, he was a loving father. Yes, I remember my mum's bruises. Still, she was telling us that she had either fallen or some domestic accidents had happened," she replied.

"Miss White, have you understood what could have triggered your brother's rage? Was he a violent brother?"

"No, Jason was very loving and even too protective of me. When Mum and Dad argued, he used to distract me and put on the music full blast, and we would dance and laugh. I do not doubt that Jason didn't mean to kill my... our Dad."

Michael decided not to question the witness, but she asked to make a statement. The judge agreed.

Anita exhaled deeply. "My mother, a few weeks before her death, came to the café where I was working at the time, wishing to talk to me. I was busy, and she had to wait 45 minutes before I could take a quick break to talk to her. She was downbeat and looked stressed. It took her a few minutes and disclaimers, as she usually does when she knows I would get annoyed. Finally, she admitted what she had done on that horrible night years ago. She confessed that after my brother had pushed and hurt my father during their confrontation... she purposefully took advantage of the situation and ended his life herself."

Gasps and murmurs exploded throughout the gallery as Anita's shocking testimony landed like a bombshell. Jason felt his heart clench as his sister's words potentially redeemed his freedom, even as they cast fresh anguish across his features.

Over the following days, Michael continued a steady push to reframe the original narrative, calling forth witnesses to attest to the cycles of turmoil within the White family, all stemming from Harry's pattern of brutal domestic abuse.

The final, crucial testimony came from the rehabilitative expert Dr Simmons. While praising Jason's efforts in counselling during incarceration, the psychologist raised some concerns.

"Mr. White has certainly made strides in confronting the roots of his trauma and rage. However, I must note that his engagement has been inconsistent and sporadic in recent months," he frowned slightly.

"There are also indications that he has developed a self-obsessive, even narcissistic tendency brought on by his cultivation of a sizable 'fan' base of enablers who I believe are disordered individuals operating under the influence of a psychological *condition* known as Hybristophilia."

"Two such individuals, a man named Jamal Adams and a young woman called Emma Wilkins, are in my professional opinion exhibiting disordered behaviours indicating they have developed a romantic obsession and non-sexual attraction to Mr White due to his status as a violent criminal. And Mr White seems to enjoy this relationship through an intense exchange of letters."

After expert rebuttals, the case was handed to the jury. It took only a couple of days to reach the verdict. The deliberations were tense before the foreperson finally read:

"The jury finds the defendant, Jason White, guilty of a lesser offence: Aggravated battery causing bodily harm against the victim, Harry White. However, in light of the new evidence indicating the identity of a possible true perpetrator and Mrs

White's indication to commit perjury, we recommend that Mr White be released from his sentence served immediately."

A wave of relief swept through Jason as the judge accepted the jury's decision and terminated his sentence. After an emotional embrace with his lawyer and friend, he stepped outside, blinking in the warm sunlight - battered and branded but gloriously free once more.

Anita had left before the verdict and left a note to Michael. Jason just put it in his jacket, and, from the stairs of the Court, surrounded by photographs and his fans holding all sorts of banners, he shouted with all the air he had in his lungs, "We are free! We are free! We made it! Justice prevailed!"

Michael, behind him, could barely contain Jason's excitement.

While he was trying to get him back inside, a young and charming lady managed to get through the crowd of photographers and reporters, hug him, and kiss him on his lips. "Emma…" that was all Jason said.

A tall, broken-hearted young man saw the scene in the crowd and could not hide his sadness. He pushed himself through the crowd and walked away from the guy he loved. This was Jamal.

The legal battle was over. While nothing could undo the violence and betrayal, Jason had regained control of his future trajectory. The path toward personal redemption was now his to travel, no matter how long or complicated the journey might be.

The decision reverberated through the internet like a shockwave in the days and weeks following his release. The *#FreeJason* movement that had rallied around his cause was now simultaneously celebrating his exoneration while turning on each other in bitter feuds.

Jason's fans attacked Dr Simmons' words. Some admitted that they were hybristophiles and proud of it, while many felt that this pathology was offensive to them and attacked with a new hashtag *#FuckYouSimmons*

Keyboard warriors took to social media, some proclaiming Jason's vindication as a hero brutalised by the system, others denouncing him as an abusive monster who belonged behind bars and that he was saved by his young sister's lies about their mother. The discourse around Jamal and Emma's blatant obsession was particularly vitriolic, with a mix of criticism and perverse fascination over their psychological conditions.

For Jamal himself, Jason's release triggered a maelstrom of turmoil. He had tied his entire sense of purpose, his very identity, to this man's incarceration and defiance of injustice. What did freedom mean for the object of his all-consuming fixation? Where did he belong in Jason's world now? Most importantly, Emma was the biggest hurdle that prevented his dreams from coming true.

Increasingly unhinged posts and videos flooded Jamal's accounts, alternating between desperate pledges of undying love and accusatory rants about Jason's supposed neglect. Consumed by the hunger of his obsession, the lines between reality and delusion blurred until all that remained was the unshakable conviction that this was his sole path to salvation—or self-immolation.

Emma's reaction was equal parts joy and despair. While her online fan communities feverishly revised their narratives to cast her as an unsung heroine who never lost faith, a creeping sense of purposelessness crept in. What would have happened if she had played her part in securing Jason's freedom? What aimless void would she spiral into without her righteous quest as a touchstone?

Anita felt a heavy regret in the wake of such a cathartic release. Their mother's dying wish would have been to secure Jason's freedom, no matter how much damage it caused in the process.

*You're out, free... but that's where it has to end for us,* Anita had scrawled, her salt-stained tears bleeding the ink in spots. *What I did, what she made me do... God forgive me. I hope that, in time, you can find peace and healing because I've lost any right to be part of that journey.*

She didn't know whether Jason had purposely killed their father or not, but she did what her mother would have wanted and helped her brother's release.

Michael Jones, for his part, felt the soul-wearying relief of having achieved hard-won victory alongside his godson. The lies, the moral falter steps, every ethically compromising decision he had made to secure this outcome—he could release it all like a long, pent-up exhalation.

He would hold no illusions about their fractured family reuniting; he would be the silent shepherd, guiding his prodigal son's first steps toward whatever path of redemption Jason chose to embrace.

Jason himself was simply numb to it all at first. The thundering roar of viral fame and infamy, the scorched earth in his life's rearview, his own sister's bitter lashing out—it was all a cacophony of well-meaning and hateful voices that he could scarcely process in those first golden weeks of freedom.

The fan groups, the obsessive artists and maligned truth-seekers, the conspiracy camps analysing his every move - he tuned them all out indifferently. Only the prospect of finally living his life unshackled by regret, without looking over his shoulder at the ghosts and false truths of his past, brought him any semblance of solace or direction.

The jail period was over. He was fundamentally unmoored, untethered from the life trajectory that imprisonment had forced upon him. The way forward would be of his own accord, for better or worse—a terrifying, seismic shift that would require the sum of all his residual willpower to accept and control.

But control was the one thing he had never truly experienced as his own. Harsh truth would be the only provision to sustain him as he stepped out to reclaim his life. All else would have to be forged entirely anew.

# Part 5 – Echoes of Justice

## 29. Back to Life

The day faded fast when Jason emerged from the courthouse, a free man for the first time in almost three years. The air had turned crisp and cold, and the fallen leaves mixed with the exhaust fumes of cars. Jason breathed, filling his lungs with the city and trying to regulate his balance between the familiar and the surreal.

Michael put a hand on his shoulder. Reporters were swarming. "Let's get you out of here," he suggested. Jason nodded. Moments later, he was led to a car. He was still shaking.

Hurtling down the avenue from the courthouse, he gazed through the car window at the liquid city streets flowing past. It was too much – the buildings, the people, the sounds. Spent, he had reverted to the being in his body as though he had been away for a long time.

Michael spoke up. "I've set up a halfway house for you to stay in for a few weeks until you return. They have work training and counselling programmes."

"You're welcome, Jason," he whispered when Jason did not react to his words.

Jason's Adam's apple bobbed as he fought back tears. "I don't know what I would've done without you. I don't know what I would've done."

Michael beamed. "Listen, kiddo, you're a tough fucking kid. You could have died, but you're still here. And it's time to start thinking about the future."

The halfway house was a utilitarian brick building between Isleworth and Twickenham on the city's fringes, not far from Chiswick. As he walked into the little, bare room that would serve as his home for the following months, it felt like *déjà vu*, like he was being returned to his cell at the prison. There was only one difference: he didn't have bars on the window.

For the first few days, he moved about in a daze, like he was reading the rhythms of life on the outside. He went to group therapy and workshops focused on job training, but he felt bored, a bit shell-shocked, and isolated. There was no sense that he or anyone around him had any direction. It seemed that these other residents were trying while he did nothing. He felt adrift.

He lay awake at night, sweating in his narrow bed with its mounting clutter of mouldy blankets, forced to replay the events that had brought him to this despair. His father was gone, murdered by his hand. His mother was dead, killed by a drunkard. Was she really his mother? His sister was lost... 'I started this chain of events. Could I ever be happy again?'

Those next several weeks were an uneasy phase during which Jason slipped into something resembling a routine. He got himself a job in a local warehouse: loading up and unloading lorries—piecework. It was hard graft, tiring mind and body, but it left him with some focus, some sense of purpose.

However, his routines made him feel like he was being watched from behind the back of his head. He sensed his skin – transparent, moving like a sailcloth as he moved. In a faint haze, he could see the gaze of other people fixed on him and their gestures beckoning him, as if he were a magnet attracting everyone's attention.

One afternoon, while leaving work, Jason saw Jamal waiting for him outside the warehouse. He had been working there for about six months as a floor supervisor, and the moment he turned the corner, he saw his biggest fan waiting for him, eyes blazing, keen, his skin vibrating with nervous energy.

"Jason," Jamal gasped, stepping toward him now. "I've been trying to contact you. I've been trying to reach you."

Jason shook his head and moved back a step. "I can't, man. I'm sorry. It won't be like this forever, Jamal," he confessed. "I can't do it. Just keep your eyes closed and think about something else." But as soon as Jamal shut his eyes, his body shuddered, and he buried his face in his hands. Jason grabbed him by the shoulders and shook him in frustration. "Man, come on! I'm trying to help out here. It won't be like this forever."

Jamal's face dropped, and his eyes brimmed with tears. "But I love you," he cried. "I have always loved you. You are the only one who understands me."

Guilt and anger charged through Jason's body. "I had a role to play in Jamal's obsession and encouraged it through the correspondence and our explorations. This was not going to turn out the way he wanted or needed. It was not going to turn out the way I wanted either," Jason would have declared sometime in the future.

"Sorry," he repeated, his voice unwavering. "I can't be in charge of your happiness now. I have to be concerned about mine."

Jamal put his head down and turned away, shoulders quaking with sobs. "Because of Emma?" he asked bitterly. "I saw the way you kissed her that day at court. Are you choosing her over me?"

"It's not Emma. Or even anyone else," was the firm reply, pushing his hair back with his right hand. "It's just me. Right now. I can't do anything else if I'm seeing anyone."

Swiping a hand to his swollen eyes, Jamal's countenance snapped taut. "Whatever. I guess I was just another sucker wise enough to fall for your bullshit. But you can bet your fine, pale ass I know precisely who you are, you sonufabitch, and I ain't never going to let you forget it."

With that, Jamal turned and walked away. Jason stood, watching him, the last of the day's light fading from behind the trees of this West London neighbourhood. There was regret in Jason's eyes and sadness over having driven Jamal away. He had wounded him and pulled back the curtain to reveal that there was no escaping his limitations as Jamal's friend and sex partner. There was no resurrecting the meek mouse that he loved. He couldn't be a hero.

The months turned to a year, and Jason took tentative steps to cobble together a new life: renting his small apartment, enrolling in classes at a community college, and going on a few nervous dates. But he'd never quite succeed in shaking free the belief that he was living on borrowed time, that the spectre of his father was always hot on his heels.

Often, he thought of Jamal and how he was taking the rejection. That his need for him was not typical, that it was a sickness, that it was based on trauma, that it was based on great grieving. And yet, what could be done? He could not fix this. Jamal might have fantasised about him, but his love was not fantastical: it was rooted deep in pain.

So, instead, he concentrated on his recovery and the slow, complex process of forgiving himself and moving on. He went to therapy, joined a survivors' support group, and volunteered at a neighbourhood centre for at-risk youth.

Gradually, he began to see that he was getting somewhere, that he was finally freeing himself from the past and felt that he might finally have a future to look forward to. And he could be right.

One night after class, he was waiting on his stoop when the woman on the steps turned out to be Jamal, skinny and hollow-eyed.

"Jamal," he said, his voice wary. "What are you doing here?"

Then Jamal lifted his face to Jason, and his eyes blazed up, filled with what could only be called a crazy look—desperate and demented all in one. "I can't stand any more of this, Jason," he gasped in a husky voice. "I can't go on without you."

Jason shivered. A feeling of foreboding welled up in him. He knew Jamal had become unbalanced –his obsession had crossed some dangerous threshold. As much as he could ignore his Social Media, it was hard not to see Jamal's rants, elucubrations and *j'accuses* about him.

"Jamal," his voice quiet but firm. "You don't need this. You can't keep doing this to yourself. Or to me."

The scorned young man gave a shake of the head. His eyes were bulging. "Understand you?" nearly shouting now. "Don't you see, sir? Only you can save me. You're the only one who can help me."

As if horrified by his move, Jason stepped away. He could feel his heart beating in his throat. He had to be careful. He had to diffuse this thing before it got hideous.

"Jamal," he uttered softly, "I can't be your messiah. I can't be the one to fix you. See, you have to do that for yourself."

Jamal's face contorted, and then he was openly sobbing, his body heaving with the force of his sorrow. He stood there looking at him, shocked, helpless.

He knew he couldn't fix Jamal, couldn't make the pain of his past go away. But he also knew he couldn't walk away, and let him suffer alone.

"Aw, dang," he said, "come here," and meekly patted him on the shoulder. They just stood there blankly for a moment—two wounded dogs. The world had gone, but one man was touching the other.

After a long pause, Jamal finally heaved himself up and wiped the tears off his face with his hand. "I'm sorry," he whispered. "I didn't mean to bring this up again, not to you, because I know you're trying to make a life for yourself."

At this, Jason only nodded; a lump suddenly constricted his throat, but he forced himself to go on. "I do. But that doesn't mean ... I mean... I want, Jamal – you to be happy and at peace – but I want that for you, not from me."

Jamal nodded solemnly, his eyes wider, like a student who had just had a profound intellectual breakthrough. "I understand now," he said. "I have so much I have to do. There is so much healing I need to do, but I am going to do it; I am going to try. I will try to be that person I know I can be."

Jason smiled, feeling a surge of pride and admiration. "I know you will, mate. And I'll be here if you need someone with your back."

The young man from Birmingham then spun around and began plodding away. The young Londoner stood there and watched him go. Hope swept over him.

'I knew my road ahead would be long and tough, that I would face so many more challenges, maybe more than I could handle,' Jason thought. 'This time, I am not alone. I have people who believe in me ... and that changes everything.'

And with that knowledge, he could walk into his apartment and deal with what came next.

He felt incomplete and emotional. Yes, he tried to move on. Like everyone else, he did his best to forget what happened. However, he couldn't overcome his sorrow over this lost family.

That night, he was sitting in his flat, piercing the blank walls of his living room with his gaze and listening to the hum of Richmond High Street outside his window, when he picked up his phone to call Anita. He was shaking lightly as he punched in the numbers.

The phone rang. Then again. Two more times. His heart pounded as he waited to hear his sister pick up, to hear her voice saying, "Hello?" But there was no ringing. Instead, the line was broken by an automated robot: "The number you have called is no longer in service."

First, Panic: 'Oh my god, something has happened!' Jason dialled again. Maybe he was off by a digit. 'Please don't let it be anything serious. Please don't let it be a mistake.' The machine answered, just like the previous time.

"Michael." He called his godfather.

"Aw, I'm sorry, Jason, but she left London a few months back, and none of us know where she went. Not even me."

Jason's stomach felt like it had been punched. "What do you mean? She left?" He was getting louder. "Why would she do that? Why wouldn't she tell me?"

A sigh came from the other side of the line. Michael's voice sounded weary. "She wasn't coping, boy. She'd been vulnerable after your parents... all that court stuff. I think she went because she needed to run away and start again someplace else."

Something in Jason combusted. "But she's my sister," he yelled, his cadence dropping. "She's all I have left. She could have waited."

And for a minute, the conversation stopped. Then: "It's hard, mate, but she went through a lot too. Her parents both died. She had to testify in court accusing her mother, to save a brother that, up to today, she doesn't know whether he killed her Dad. You know."

Jason felt guilt shoot through his heart for the first time. He knew Michael was right that Anita had suffered as much as he had done. But knowing it didn't help him. He shut his eyes tight, trying to block out the misery in his soul.

"Please, do you know where she is?" he asked, his voice small and hopeful.

Michael hesitated, and Jason could hear the conflict in his voice. "I'm sorry, Jason. To tell the truth, I promised Anita I wouldn't tell anyone where she was going. She needs to heal; she needs to find her way."

He sank to the floor and felt as if he were falling into the midst of a sucking, turbulent sea, his spirits sinking as surely as his body, heavier, more profound, dragged helplessly among the raging waves, drifting, bobbing and sinking, left to die, alone amid death on the dark sea.

But then Michael's voice cut through his grief for him: "You know, there's more in this. Your father... in his will, something was left for you."

Jason's spine shivered with surprise. "Money?" he said. "How much?"

"Seven hundred and fifty thousand pounds," Michael said softly. "From when the house sold and from your father's life insurance policy. He wanted you to have it, but there are terms and conditions."

Deep down, the young man felt something flicker inside him. His father was still trying to rule him, even in the grave, trying to dictate the terms on which he lived his life. "What kind of conditions, then?" he asked defiantly.

"He wanted you to get a real job," was the answer. "He wanted you to hold on to it for several years. He thought you'd get into the swing of things. He thought giving you a routine would help you sort yourself out."

Jason laughed, a dry, bitter sound. "A future. What sort of future can I have after what's passed?"

Michael's voice was insistent as if to offer him quiet yet wholesome encouragement to pick up the pieces: "A good one, man. A potential where you can be happy and have peace of mind but have to work for it and earn it."

Jason was quiet for a tense moment.

That was also something he must carry with him for the rest of his life, making this discovery, an unwelcome gift—to have his father's love, even in the grave, bound up with conditions.

"I don't know if I can..." he stated, his voice discreet. "I don't know if I can do it. I'm not sure I'm strong enough."

"You are," was the answer. "You've overcome so much already. You've come so far. You can do this too. And I'll be here to help you... every step."

Jason felt grateful as he realised his friend was right. He had to keep moving and keep fighting for the life he wanted.

"Okay," he confirmed, his voice shaking slightly. "I'll try, mate. I'll do my best."

"That's all anyone can ask, mate! Just that. And know that you're not alone. People care about you and believe in you. And we'll be here, OK?"

The sense of closure he felt after that phone call pulled Jason back to his feet as he stood in his kitchen.

He thought of Anita, the sister who had been lost to him, and their losses that could never be made good. He might never see her again.

But he also knew that he needed to keep going and fighting for the life he wanted, and he would do it. He would keep trying, not just for himself but for the family he'd lost and for the family he might one day have.

Taken aback, he exhaled and went to the window. Beyond the glass, the High Street spread out before him, buzzing with people.

Interestingly, a few weeks after his unsettling meeting with Jamal, he was greeted by an email from Emma in his inbox that Wednesday morning. He opened the message, and then his heart rate speeded.

*Dear Jason,*

*Kindly let me know if it reaches you well. After our kiss outside the Courthouse the other day, I kept thinking of you. So, I mean, you and I haven't talked since we both got caught up in the whirlwind of that day at the trial. But that doesn't mean for one second that I've stopped being concerned about your well-being.*

*I'm coming to London this weekend for a friend of mine. I wondered if we could hang out, have dinner, and catch up. I totally get it if you are not ready to see anyone from that era of your life. However, if you're open, I'd love to talk with you in person to know how you are doing.*

*Let me know if you're free. I am going to stay in Kensington.*
*Wishing you all the best,*
*Emma*

He read the email on his screen, a turmoil of mixed feelings blooming in his chest. While unable to help a spark of warmth at the thoughtfulness shown towards him by Emma, those feelings were quickly overshadowed once more by his only fear: this rekindling was once again reopening the doors to his past that he had worked so hard to close. There was a part of him who hoped to dismiss the development.

But another part of him hungered for the kind of insight and camaraderie Emma always gave him, even from afar. She was one of his staunchest defenders, and the meet-up that day outside the court suggested they might have more in common than he had initially thought.

Jason took a deep breath and then replied.

*Hi Emma,*

*It's great to hear from you! I'd like to see you too. That is so nice. Dinner works for me; let me know when and where. I can't wait.*
*-Jason*

He sat at a cosy Italian restaurant in Kensington on Saturday evening, tapping his foot irritably. On the other hand, Emma did not resemble being a life-long social media warrior. He was immediately taken aback by how she looked compared to the person he had been used to seeing fire off so many tweets and Facebook since he was acquitted and had access to a PC again. There was something that seemed gentler, naively vulnerable, about her in person and never entirely captured through a computer screen.

In no time, with their wine glasses in hand, the awkwardness of first impressions dissolved into a correct-the-record airing. Both described the emptiness, aimlessness and struggle to reclaim an everyday life after the trial. "It completely unravelled everything I knew to be true in my world," he confessed gingerly, talking about hybristophilia.

She nodded. "Oh ya... I believe that how I felt about you was probably pretty unhealthy for me." She admitted. "Sure, a lot of allure came from the drama and how 'forbidden' it all was. Okay, well, for the record, I actually cared about you as a person. That part was always real."

As the evening progressed and wine got poured, it was impossible not to feel that something was going on between them. Or maybe it was the ongoing talk or how he knew first-hand what drove her to such unreasonable heights?

When he wanted to return to his in Richmond, she thought absolutely. They jumped in a Uber, holding hands and exchanging nervous glances and timid smiles.

In Jason's apartment, the festering high finally exploded into full-blown passion. There was some escapism in it, too, some of losing yourself in the physical connection to make past hurts not hurt so much. But it was gentler, too, like two hearts that had been broken finding kindness in one another.

In the afterglow, he drew lazy little circles on her bare shoulder and repeated over and over to himself how incredible it was that 'this had happened tonight.' But he also sensed their journey together was less than secure—for both of them, there were still so many wounds left to mend.

But after so long, he dared to hope again. Dared believe that maybe, just maybe, he wasn't the only one out there. He smiled and pulled Emma closer before letting his body rest and gently drift off into slumber.

Once she settled with him in his flat in Richmond and started looking for work in London, they were in a kind of newlywed domestic harmony—getting up together in the morning, sharing meals—which they might have always craved after spending all that time apart. After all these years, Jason revelled in the simple pleasures of living with a woman in a family *menage*.

But with time – months– little fault lines had started to crack into their relationship. She continued to run the Jason White fan pages months after news of the murder faded from the headlines. One evening, she casually mentioned, over dinner, that she had made thousands of pounds from donations and advertising revenue while he was fighting his court case.

"People kept giving, and I could fund my living expenses and tuition through this." This was Emma's Only Fans, a membership site offering free and paid content. At the start of her video, she's seated before her webcam. Behind her, the flat was mostly bare, with only one wall adorned with posters. She greeted her viewers with a "Hey" and began her spiel. "I am so excited to be with you today," she would say. "I thought I'd start by showing you... my boobs." But then she would talk seriously about the Jason White case, giving her and his fans updates about the prisoner and reading his letters to her and her fans. She was brilliant and sold those letters to a limited group. She used it as a magnet to attract money and increase her popularity among other free groups to benefit from paid advertising. She had put on a big circus and monetised it.

Jason practically stopped chewing pasta. "Did you say you've been living off money from my case? Selling my letters on the web?"

"That's not how it is," she blazed; "you don't get it! I was so busy moderating groups like that, keeping them going, making people do their jobs, and fighting for their freedom that it was a full-time job."

"But it doesn't seem right, making a profit off my tragedy," he insisted. "That money should go to some charity, some legal defence fund for people who were wrongly convicted like me."

"Pardon me?" she flashed anger in her eyes. "I'm entitled to payment for my innumerable hours on this. If not for my handiwork, you'd probably be rotting in jail."

The sharp reminder of his incarceration made him cringe. "I'm grateful for everything you did, Emma. But this changes the way I think about it. It's like it puts the pure desire in a bad light. I almost feel that it poisons it."

She shifted forward on her chair and inched closer until her knees brushed against his. "How dare you throw these allegations at me?" she yelled. "I was unafraid to stand by you. I left everything behind me for your sake."

With their voices rising in acrimony, Jason suddenly realised that this was the first real fight he and his new partner had had together. The money issue had exposed more primitive anxieties and doubts—was he okay with Emma, or were 'the two of us living under a species of delusion enabled by something extraordinary?'

A frosty tension hung over the apartment for the next few days. Emma obsessively applied to jobs, and Jason withdrew into long, brooding silences. They circled each other like satellites, warily exchanging short sentences, both lightly gloved, slowly retreating into separate worlds of icy romance.

He woke up in the middle of the night, and the bed was empty. Huddled over her laptop in the living room, she pulled her sweatshirt up to her ears, her face glistening with fresh tears. He took the seat next to her and pulled her to him.

"I'm sorry for being judgemental," he murmured into her hair. "It's just that I know your heart was in the right place. It's all so new and so much."

She sighed and nuzzled into him. "I am sorry, too. I should have been more upfront about the money. I was terrified of bursting this bubble we've been living in."

Together, they clung to each other in the dark, aware that putting a life together would be more complicated than they thought. The idealised tale of their love gave way to the realities of two complex people finally combining their scars and well-stored baggage.

But even in that storm of doubt and growing pains, there was a glimmer of optimism. With tolerance, communication, and guts enough to chase down their inner demons, they might rise above their tabloid soap opera characters to become simply the man and woman they had hoped to be beneath the caricatures.

As images of Jason and Emma's 'jet-set' lifestyle began to emerge via their social media channels, the fans' adoration turned to abuse, and, for a while, the couple became the centre of a concerted and vicious online hate campaign. Comment threads and discussion forums reported on the sad story of a trusting girl dragged down the wrong path, accused the pair of making money out of a tragedy, asked *Why didn't Jason care if Jamal was gay, and ignored him once he was out.* Some even suggested that it might be nice if both of them committed suicide.

*It's all charity money, and we pay for their dinners, trips, and holidays. We believed in Jason's innocence, but it's a con; he is a con.* One former donor and supporter objected.

Jamal led the charge, seething over Jason's rejection – and Emma's evident happiness – and flooding the message boards demanding a full accounting of donations, threatening to sue her if she couldn't prove where every penny went.

"If you ain't got nothin' to hide, show me your receipts!" He shouted in the vitriolic Instagram Reel. "Or are you offsetting all that money into your bank account?"

The couple at the centre of the storm never saw that attack coming.

One evening, around midnight, they sat together at the kitchen table with their heads in their hands, trying to think through their options.

"I never meant for it to look as though we were profiting from people's goodwill," she said, her voice cracking. "I thought I was doing the right thing, using those sums to keep the thing going and paying some of the bills myself."

He pulled a long sigh. "I know, love. But perception is everything. And right now, it doesn't look good. It doesn't look very good. We have to do something before this turns into a full-fledged scandal."

An idea began to coalesce in his thoughts. "What if we had Michael Jones announce that a decent portion of the money had been spent on his legal fees for the retrial? It would explain where good part of the money had been paid and that it had been spent for its supposed purpose, his professional fees."

Emma was chewing her lip a bit. "Yeah. Maybe. But it would mean... we are putting Michael in an awkward position, like asking him to be our alibi. And, let's be honest, we are asking him to lie."

"He's always been pretty good watching out for me," he reassured her, more surety in his voice than he felt. "He'll know what to do."

The two returned to Michael's Isle of Dogs office in East London the next day. They explained the predicament and recommended their solution. His expression didn't change, but the faintest note of disappointment rippled in his eyes.

"Okay, what are you suggesting?" he questioned, trying to slow his escalating anger. "I should say that a lot of the money collected from the fans went toward your retrial expenses when we both know it isn't true?"

Jason squirmed where he sat. "I hate to have to ask you this, Michael. But we don't have much time. If we can't show where the money went, it might end everything we've worked for."

"I've stood by you," the lawyer affirmed, steepling his fingers. "I believed in your innocence. I believe in your right to put your life back together again. But this..." He shook his head.

He took a deep breath, and his shoulders slumped. "Fine," he concluded, "here's what I will do. I will say something about the expenses. But you should know, generally, I am not comfortable with this. I am afraid you are missing the trees for the forest. You could come out clean, Emma, and say, 'I will pay the money back. I needed it to run the campaign while out of work'. It would not differ from the lie you are asking me to say. But, ok, I shall do it. I leave the matter between you two as I do not want to get into the details. How much are we talking about?"

Relief mingled with guilt warmed the young couple's faces as they thanked the friend repeatedly. But as they walked out of the office, heads bowed, hands clasped, a dark feeling persisted.

Was there something evil about their attempt to shield themselves from the judgment of that mob? How many more lies would it take to preserve the goal of a fairytale?

In the heaving view of Canary Wharf and the City of London, the skyline stretching out forward, the two pressed into one another collusively, feeling, as they each did separately, that their hard-won union sat precariously on sands, where compromises had been smuggled under moral verities.

Jason was thoughtful and questioned himself and his relationship with Emma. There were too many lies and complications, and, most importantly, the roots were still too clenched into the past.

With Michael's public letter of explanation, they managed to subdue most supporters, who were content that most of the money donated to the cause had been spent on Jason's legal case. The fact that Emma admitted to paying a 'few' thousand pounds on rogue press without a receipt felt like a small error in an otherwise damage-limiting accounting.

Yet one or two sceptics remained unconvinced. Besides, it didn't seem likely that a true friend would take such a massive fee to defend his godson. Pushed on this point, Michael issued another statement:

*I stopped taking on every other client and case – each of which took time, effort and money to progress – while I took on Jason's case. The £30,000 from the donations represents barely a tenth of the earnings I lost through dropping everything for his defence. I gave freely of everything I had – and I am immensely proud of having* done so. It might be different in America, where an elite cadre of well-compensated lawyers lap up the lucrative business that has thrown their way. Still, lawyers are much less likely to fall into that trap in England (and, I believe, continental Europe). Yet I had to reimburse myself in my name for my living expenses and the costs of building up Jason's defence.

For everyone else, after hearing his justification, the issue was put to bed. Most people understood the circumstances and could see that Michael was devoting his time to a cause he believed in, even at a significant personal financial cost.

However, Jamal was still smarting from romantic rejection, jealous over Jason and Emma's relationship, and energised into creating a new Facebook group: *Unmasking the Truth: The Jason White Fraud*.

This was the forum where he and a couple of other disaffected former fans dismantled every word that Emma and Michael published, scrutinising every letter and disbelieving any statement they saw as inconsistent. They pored over Instagram and Facebook photos, suggesting that the luxury hotel rooms and fancy meals photographed by the sweethearts proved that the pair were enjoying the high life off the backs of their supporters. He, a warehouse manager, and she, an unemployed student, could not afford such a lifestyle.

His posts turned more belligerent, malicious, and full of paranoid speculation about everything. He alleged that Emma, aka the Mantis, was a manipulative gold-digger and that Jason was a willing accomplice who turned a blind eye to her behaviour. He even claimed that Jason was guilty from the first and that the conviction had only been avoided because he had manipulated the legal system through his godfather's silver-spooned lawyers and coerced his sister into perjury.

At first, the couple tried to brush the group off, pretending it never happened or rationalising it as the sighs of a jilted fan with an axe to grind. But as Jamal's followers grew and his outrage became more inflammatory, they began to show signs of fatigue.

As she became increasingly irritated at him, Emma lay in bed late at night, scrolling through the last updates on her denigrator's page, staring at the hard light from his phone.

"They're never going to drop this, are they?" she asked symbolically. "Whatever we say, whatever we do, they'll always find some way to turn it against us."

Jason drew her to him and kissed her forehead. "I know it's hard. It's hard for me too. But we have to hang on to what's real. Here's what's real: we know what happened, and so do the people who count. The rest is just noise."

And though he went on to say all the right things, Jason couldn't help but feel deflated. 'How long can we keep this up, protect ourselves against suspicion and scrutiny, and defend our every move and joy before we evolve into something we don't recognise?'

Together, they lived, dreamed, and loved. But each night, as sleep arrived, the poison of Jamal's obsession descended like a smothering fog. It threatened to swirl into their happiest moments and destroy them. Both would hope, though, that there would come a day when this nightmare storm would pass when they would have survived the elements and emerged as tougher, tempered, more meaningful creatures in each other's arms.

Yet the jeopardy lurking in the basement of their attachment was an underlying suspicion, however unwelcome: that the very qualities that drew them together—their fiery intensity—might, after all, also be their ruination, a two-edged sword that hurt as intensely as it had healed.

Emma could tell Jason had other plans. One evening, her fork jangled against the plate, and she looked at him in disbelief. The £25,000 secret fund, left over from her fan donations, was a kind of insurance policy against her and Jason's shared future.

"And you want me to take our money and just hand it to people? After all I've done? After all I've given up? Just give it to some people who didn't even bother working for it?" she said, getting pretty worked up.

Jason blew out an exasperated breath and raked a hand through his hair. "Look, I understand what you're saying, but this thing cannot stay buried, or Jamal and the others will never stop harassing us, not as long as they think we have something to hide. And giving that money away tells them we aren't after them for our profit."

"Greed, surely?" She snapped. "I worked years and years for you. I put my heart and soul into it, and now you'll be wealthy with your inheritance. Suddenly, the money I've earned turns bad while your inheritance from the father you hated and wanted dead is good?"

She rose to her feet, her eyes flashing with anger and hurt. "Sometimes, I think... I wish... you'd still been in prison. At least back then, you were an image, a cause. This new you, the one who will sell me down the river for a load of journalistic hyenas? You're just a spineless pussy."

His temper flared, too. "Perhaps I was right not to trust you; perhaps I did have reason to think that you were drawn to my dark side, and that's what you fell in love with. Because that's the side you see, not my normal side, which is trying to build a life for myself, and I can't do that if you don't stop hurting me with the past."

She flinched as though he had hit her. "Who the fuck are you to tell me I didn't love you? The way you acted, you could have spent the rest of your worthless life in prison, but I waited for you, bitched up for you. And maybe they were right. Maybe you're a fantasist, and I loved nothing but a charade."

She grabbed her coat and her handbag. Her hands shook with fury and loss. "Sure, start a new life. Just do it entirely without me. I am sick and fucking tired of being your sandbag for violence and your box for every misery of living."

When she stormed out of the flat and slammed the door behind her, Jason collapsed into a chair, his head in his hands. The past nearly half-decade's pain and remorse felt like an engine boiling over.

His mind drifted for a moment to the life he'd left behind – to the family that had been taken from him. If only, he thought, he had the chance to change the decisions he'd made, to be the brother and son to them that they'd needed.

But that life was over, broken forever by a single irredeemable act of violence, and now here was Emma gone to follow it, and he felt lonelier than ever, roaming the earth drifting on waves of unforgettable guilt.

When the slanting light of morning fell through the curtains, cold and keen, making dark pools across what was now the bare room, Jason wondered if there would come a time when he could stop paying for what he'd done, a time when he might learn that redemption was not a mocking figment, quickly snatched away just as he thought he might finally take hold of it.

He picked up his phone and searched his contacts until he found Michael's number. If anyone could help restore his life, it was his godfather, the only father figure in a life of loss and upheaval.

Following the social-media war between Emma and Jamal, Jason's original fan base split into bickering tribes that all claimed the moral elevation that came from having never fallen for the capitalist snake oil in the first place.

Among Emma's supporters, Jason's portrayal of the romantic turned topsy-turvy as he was seen as the witless coward who'd exploited Emma's devotion to escape prison and then dropped her the moment she no longer suited him. Streams of social media comments poured across Instagram and Facebook featuring memes satirising Jason's short man syndrome, suggesting that he'd only killed his father by accidentally sneezing.

So Emma herself became the inspiration for much commentary, the source of biting aside about Jason's character and motives. She was described as a weak woman who had deceived herself about a man's true nature; she had allowed herself to be wooed into a relationship; she had put Jason on a pedestal and stayed there too long.

Across the chasm, members of Jamal's camp seized on the split to support their contention that Jason was a sham all along – a confidence trickster who had fooled Emma with a sob story of tragic pathology and heroic rehabilitation and had deceived the public the same way. The turn against him that Emma had made was but proof of what Jamal and his colleagues had been saying all along.

He continued to contact Jason, trying to schedule an interview or be quoted in a statement about what had happened. Still, Jason refused to participate in the media circus that his life had become.

So the influencer put out a public 'timer' on the days since he had reached out to Jason, with the radio silence used as ammo for a series of increasingly hostile accusations of cowardice and dishonesty.

Emma happily contributed her bite to this campaign. Everyone around her seemed to take a perverse pleasure in tearing down the man she had loved, as if burning down his likeness might redeem the extent of her past obsession and ease her current pains.

Month by month, the online feud would morph into an autoimmune feedback loop of heat, hate, outrage and poison, a two-headed monster of the former hybristophiles racing to the bottom of the emotional pile, each vying to be the most swindled, the most betrayed by the subject of their mutual fixation.

Lost in the jamboree was any sense of proportion or generosity of spirit, any acknowledgement of the participants' chains of trauma and guilt, sorrow and bewildered aspiration. Jason had become an empty screen on which Jamal and Emma could project their anxieties and insecurity and betrayed visions of romance and redemption.

And all along, Jason was there, saying nothing, a silent apparition in the long vortex of noise that enveloped him. He had gone away into the peace of work and study, into the heartache of his own dark and unspoken self-assessment.

At its worst, he wondered if this would be all he was remembered for – not the ghastly saga of a son driven over the edge, but a cautionary fable of a man who had become a puppet animatronic for the grandiose delusions of others, an icon of the dangers of celebrity and notoriety on the web.

As the weeks became months and the fury subsided, he could only hope there might be a day when he could recover the narrative of his life, repossess his story and tell it, adequately contextualised, on his terms.

For now, he endured, burdened by his shame and with the knowledge that, for all that he'd caused and even the mess he'd just made of his life, he was still just a person – fallible and limited, and still learning the lay of a nightscape that had never been agreeable to dreamers.

During the twelve months since Emma's exit, he had doused a sagging significance with the soaps of service and self-betterment. His father had left him wealthy enough to live a quiet, undubbed, identity-free existence, unburdened by the need to over-achieve, impress, graduate, pass, rehabilitate, or prosper, unbound by commitments other than to himself.

He'd bought a small, terraced house in South Ealing, where most of his modest fortune went into establishing a home that felt secure. The rest of the money went to a financial adviser who helped him build up a portfolio of investments that would provide him passive earnings for the rest of his life – money that would enable him never to have to concern himself about basic living expenses again.

Since his release from prison, he worked at the same warehouse —where he'd become a manager, proving himself with natural leadership and a strong work ethic among a staff who looked up to him. He found meaning in honest work, in pushing boxes, in belonging to the team and in the team belonging to him.

However, it was only when he began volunteering at a mental health charity that he felt fulfilled. He threw himself into helping young people who were coping with similar feelings of loneliness, fury, and hopelessness as he had once been. He reassured them that he had been there and his life had been transformed. He delivered his story as an inspiring tale, not a morality lesson.

Their ability to help more children and families seemed to grow exponentially as his donations were used to expand the charity's waiting lists and services. "I can now actually use my inherited money for good," he said one day during a meeting with less advantaged kids. "It's why I've become so compulsive about giving, I suppose, to those less fortunate." But not much less. The shame of being branded with the inherited militia stigma and the accompanying erosion of respect that accompanied it had not just lifted – it had been replaced with a sense of satisfaction.

But even in his new life, he occasionally felt the pangs of loneliness. Anita, Mike, and others were all gone now. He had no idea where any of them were. To him, they might as well have vanished from the planet.

By then he didn't even have a social media presence – he just had an email address and a mobile phone with no internet access. He had refused interviews from papers and TV networks in his effort to let the past go. He had learned the lesson of living your life 'out there', as he called it, where you were subject to everyone and their opinions about you.

Instead, his addiction was to a small circle of trusted acquaintances and colleagues, for whom he was known not as a tabloid pantomime villain or a source of morbid curiosity but as the man he was at that moment. He enjoyed sitting at home reading or pottering about in a small garden. He liked walking along tree-lined suburban streets of Northfields Avenue and Lammas Park, inhaling the anonymity and quiet greeting unknown by-passers in the morning.

Of course, sometimes the ghosts of the past were still with him: the occasional glimmering of his mother's smile or a gnawing of conscience at the errors he'd made with Emma. But he had gained the wisdom to dispense with them in memory rather than being kicked in the guts by them in the present. He would have to live knowing that his journey would always be about redemption, not sainthood.

*And that is what a man does: with a modest stillness, with a quiet sense of being shared by others, he takes each day as a gift, grateful to have arrived safely, thankful to be useful, grateful to have the variable maze of the moment still ahead of him, eager to re-engage with the slow, blessed, labour of making something he can be proud of – all over again.* He wrote once while sitting on the top deck of a bus heading towards Richmond Park for the day.

A full five years had passed since that night when Jason's world had been painfully ripped away. In the interim, he had recalibrated and steeled himself. Biweekly psychotherapeutic counselling, a job he loved at the warehouse, and working for charities —his investments and a small mortgage, all afforded him a sustained life.

But by carefully heeding his therapist's advice and refraining from using social media altogether, he was determined to make sure he didn't get pulled back into the swirling cauldron of his past. Returning to Facebook or even reading the posts, without a doubt, would have opened the floodgates again and left him once more with his feet planted firmly back in quicksand.

Meanwhile, the storm across the sea of bits and bytes raged on just as fiercely. Though they could agree on at least one thing – their shared sense of grievance –Jamal and Emma remained bitterly at odds, with the former repeatedly accusing Emma of co-opting her relationship with the 'star' Jason for personal attention and profit. He inspired yet more hatred towards Emma from his supporters.

The furore over supposed money theft had largely died down. Jamal's ultimatum countdown for Jason – which once generated dozens of new comments an hour – now languished at the bottom of the page, unconverted, with no new comments or interaction. From that day on, the two hybristophiles had essentially created a safe space – a hermetically sealed echo chamber that, as soon as someone within shouted something that didn't align with the narrative they were propagating, relentlessly silenced it.

Eventually, the public's appetite for Jason's story petered out, too. The people who once had their eyes glued to every twist and turn of his story, swooning and wailing, had moved on to new scandals. New heroes and villains to lionise and crucify. The memes and hashtags that had once scrolled up and down Twitter and Facebook feeds vanished and were replaced by newer viral memes.

In this obscurity, Jason had his relief—no longer under the microscope, subject to endless speculation and gossip, he was free to address his healing process to redefine his identity. His life was increasingly structured by simple rhythms—the physicality of the work in the warehouse, the quiet conversations he had with suicidal youths at the charity, and the conversations he had with his therapist about his heart. It slowly coalesced into a new self, independent of the spectacle he'd become.

While the scars of his traumas could never be wholly eradicated, through excruciating exertion, he'd learned to submit to the healing process and find peace in the imperfect moments of the present instead of being dragged inexorably towards the ghosts of a troubled past. A transformation can never be complete; it's a lifelong engagement with being the best version of yourself that you can be, one step at a time.

If he was embodying this lesson, it was because he had found calm in his neat little house – at his quiet address, in the wide robustness of the streets he had chosen. He had found calm because he had come to appreciate every sunrise, every chance to deposit in the bank of harmlessness, however small.

In the direction of his destiny, he knew that things would still go wrong, that he would still falter, shake his fist at the sky. But if he could still open his wounds and unpack all the debris, if he could still see the purity of the stars in the few eyes of those who could look past his façade, if he could still stand beneath the gaze of his night sky, then perhaps he would have everything he needed.

The world might have moved on from Jason White, but for the former inmate, his story's best part was just beginning. It was the quiet tale of redemption, calm and common decency rising from the abyss of unthinkable horror. It was a tale that would never be read in broadsheets or retweeted, but it was one that the ex-con was proud to say was his for the first time in his life.

## 30. *Emma*

Emma remained rudderless in the ugly mess that followed Jason's breakup, still pulling at the delusional instincts that drove her obsession with his case. The dizzying heat of her adoration for Jason had cooled into an acid taste of betrayal.

At first, she vented her grief by posting more messages in the cyber squabble with Jamal, attempting to come up with the most damning ripostes, and trying to gather her allies to her side. The digital battlefield helped to keep the inevitable grief at bay; it also helped distract her from the emptiness that Jason's absence had left in her life.

However, as the months rolled on, the bright artificial glow of the likes that followed her posts online began to feel like an increasingly flimsy substitute for the warm affirmations of the flesh-and-blood people in her life.

As quiet spread and the light from the screen dimmed, silences stretched and feeds withered. The illusions of security and self-worth she had so strenuously clung to evaporated, and Emma realised that she had constructed a disastrous fiction. This fantasy had become self-deception, to which her identity and sense of worthiness were perfectly aligned.

For her as a hybristophile, Jason's dark, dangerous shadows and the taboo enjoyment of rooting for the undesired took precedence over a deep love for him. But under the harsh glare of the every day, she wondered if she was attracted to Jason, the man or the fictional Jason she'd imagined.

She searched for solace and meaning, finding her way into communities and online discussion forums devoted to hybristophilia, where those suffering from the passion could share their stories. She found a peculiar comfort in the tales of those who had experienced an all-encompassing obsession with the deviant; these individuals were like her.

Still, she wasn't one of the hybristophiles whose lives and intellect teemed with activity, even as she connected with her new kin. A consuming sense of emptiness still plagued her. The colossal psychic effort expended in her adoration of Jason had left her spirit seriously drained, and she was unable to form normal, healthy relationships or find purpose in her life beyond the ecstatic worship of a 'dead' man.

Her grades continued to fall, her few friendships withered, and her bright light of a personality faded as she grew disenchanted about what she had gotten involved with. The things that had initially attracted her to Jason — his darkness, his rich contradiction, his disregard for the rules and conventions of the world — came to stand as painful acknowledgements of her dogged idealism.

At her very lowest ebb, when she remembered her devotion to Jason and all it brought to her life, she missed that deep sense of meaning and connection. The excitement of the chase, the comfort of righteousness in the face of opposition — the kind of manic, intoxicated feeling of belonging to something bigger than herself: these were the drugs of which she was in need, the voids to which she longed to be addicted.

But over time, and as the wounds opened up by her lover's duplicity began to heal, she started to understand that an enduring sense of wholeness would not come as a byproduct of someone else's. She would have to forge her own story to find worth and self-definition outside the context of her hybristophilia.

With the help of a therapist who counselled paraphilic disorders, she began a long trip of disentangling the genesis of her allure towards those who had been branded criminals. She had dug up her trauma, the wounds that remained raw, and she was taking strides to remove the foundations of her deviance.

Yet, this quest for self-discovery led her to rediscover pieces of herself and develop curiosities and passions that were uniquely her own. She took to writing, penning emotional essays and short stories that explored the enigmas of the human subconscious.

Even with the pull of hybristophilia still there at the edges of her mind, through analgesia into anaesthesia, she learned that the path to cure and wellness was not the forbidden but the authentic self.

Throughout her journey of self-conscious recollection, beyond pain and disillusionment, beyond voice, judgment and control, essay and closure, she arrived at a story: her own. This story was one of unspeakable sorrow, but it was also one of flourishing, of wrenching herself free from the grip of an obsessive bond with this destructive force and becoming, through it, stronger and better and determined to live the life she deserved.

Though she would forever bear the marks of her past, Emma, now empowered, wouldn't be confined by them. She wanted to use what she'd gone through to show others that they weren't alone: to understand the pain another person had gone through, to empathise is to be vulnerable. *I want to be a voice in a crowd of people who also have depression and can relate*, she wrote in one of her short stories.

Eventually – and only eventually – she developed a new form of connectedness, not with a remorseless psychopath, but with the warm, messy, lifelong intimacy of genuine human relationships. She filled her orbit with friends and family who cherished her not for her innocently vulnerable allure – nor for her deep, dark wells of cruelty – but as the inconsistent, frail, quirky, flawed, wise and generous being she could now be.

Her hybristophilia was not a cautionary or humiliating tale but proof of the soul's ability to resist its expression. Though her affair with Jason had reached a tragic end, she knew the rest of her story was yet to be written—a tale of triumph, healing, and the endless opportunities open to a life lived freely.

She sat still, the letter from Anita shaking in her hands as the words inside it began to sink in. She could no longer read them, but that in no way lessened their meaning: Anita had been lying on the stand; Jason, even more surely than his mother, had murdered. His sister had done it because she believed she was fulfilling Germaine's last dying wish. She wanted her son freed.

Emma was awhirl with emotions—shock, anger, and a feeling of sickening betrayal. She maintained her belief in Jason's innocence and fought to free him. She had invested everything in mounting his defence and found out that the foundation of his release was a lie.

As the initial shock faded, a more nefarious urge started to take over. The ancient pull of hybristophilia, prompted a wave of excitement deep in her soul. The knowledge that Jason did, indeed, get away with murder, that the system had failed to hold him accountable, aroused the same sickening thrill she thought had long disappeared.

For days, she tallied up the competing sides in the endless battle of her inner landscape. On the one hand, 'I've come so far, worked so hard, and had such a long time undoing all that destructive stuff, building myself a life worth living. It's all been for nothing. I'll have squandered all that hard work, all those chances to live a sane life, to one last manic afternoon in front of my PC. I'd have pedalled it all away.' Meanwhile, something stirred deep in her dark place.

But still, the lure was there. The thought of outing Jason, of seeing the residents of the zeitgeist turn from adoration to outrage, was heady. She pictured how the media attention would swell, how her hordes of faceless fans would return to worship at her feet, label her an avenging angel, a bringer of righteousness.

She let herself imagine how good it would feel, how right it would be, to see him tumbling down, to see him thrown back into the cell where he belonged, to reverse all the torments he had inflicted upon her, proving all the lies, the deceptions she had endured. The urge to bury him in her bitterness only grew greater. It was like a hungry beast biting away deep within her innards.

Yet, as she indulged in hybristophilic fantasies, she also retained a fragment of sanity. While wallowing in revenge-related arousal might provide a temporary outlet, she knew that surrendering to her hybristophilic urges wouldn't give the release she sought. She read from experts that pressing forward would only reignite her pain, drawing her back into the vortex of obsessive mania and self-destructive despair that threatens the very existence of hybristophiles.

Caught between her vengeful desires and perhaps reconnecting with a criminal once he had been thrown in jail and the healing she had worked so hard to obtain, she faced a choice. She could hold on to the past, to the dynamics of hatred that had deprived her of human connection and love for so long, or she could embrace the future and continue to take new steps on the road to recovery and self-discovery.

In the end, however, it was what she had to lose that allowed her to rise above the pull of the strips—the people she loved and their love for her, the writing she was able to produce, the advocacy and the laughter that meant so much to her, the capacity for resilience that had grown in her over the years, and the sense of meaning she found in it all.

Her grief was such that she thought of folding up the letter, creeping to the confines of her fireplace, and burning the words of words. Emma's fire became a living door into another form of 'reality' – at once a symbolic space of unashamedly creative closure and a literal space of comforting intimacy. Finally, her hand steady and tears wiped from her face, she watched as the darkened pages curled and hurled in flames – blackened characters twisting on themselves into soot and smoke.

Once the last embers had been extinguished, Emma would have felt a sense of catharsis.

But that idea was quickly rejected.

When she decided to air Anita's letter, she would have triggered another revival of Jason's case, pummelling the story across the media. She promised an explosive announcement on her relaunched OnlyFans channel, including a whole letter reading.

As the moment approached, the internet filled with rumours. People eagerly joined in the speculation, wondering if we'd crank up the intrigue and complexity another notch.

For her, those were dramatic days. But she wanted revenge, and deep down, she hoped to find her Jason again.

Ten thousand viewers—the queue to get into the show extended for several minutes—paid the £7 entry fee to log on to Emma's OnlyFans page; this was the moment the case that had made Jason White a household name came crashing to a conclusion. The chat box was abuzz with speculation, and Jason White fans worldwide traded theories, asking one another what they expected her to reveal.

The clip came on at the appointed moment, and Emma's face came on the screen, looking sad, matter-of-fact and resolute. She gave a little sigh, her eyes on camera, and started reading:

"Good evening, folks, and welcome to tonight's show. Whatever I have to tell you will rattle your beliefs to its core — never again will there be a moment's doubt about what happened in that terrible tale, the Jason White case."

Her tone was calm, but a tremor in her voice revealed how serious this was. She grabbed a piece of paper from a desk and held it before the camera.

"This is a letter from Anita White, Jason's sister, saying she lied on the stand. She falsely accused her mother of murdering her father, which had sent Jason to prison for a crime he deservedly committed."

When she began to read the letter out loud, the chat exploded in seismic reaction. Messages bombarded the window, with fans expressing confusion, shock, disbelief, and anger.

*I can't believe it! Jason was guilty all along!*
*How could Anita lie like that to get her brother out of prison?*
*This changes everything. Jason needs to be locked up again!*

A few viewers started calling for the young man to be re-arrested and returned to prison to finish serving his sentence.

One user's claim struck at the heart of this issue: *If Jason is back in jail because the lady perjured herself, he should never have been out in the first place! This is a travesty of justice. Jason got away with murder!*

While reading, Emma began to feel her sorrow: her voice shook, tears welled in her eyes as she recalled details about the deceptions and betrayals that allowed Jason to have his freedom. To win the game, she wanted him dead. For her, this moment was not just about truth. It was about achieving a kind of justice.

However, in the face of outrage and demands of vengeance, Jason White still found an audience. Some of his fans initially refused to believe the letter's contents and claimed that his ex girlfriend had fabricated the evidence to ruin his reputation.

*I don't believe her. Emma is just being a bitch because Jason dumped her.*

*This letter could be a fake. I still believe in Jason's innocence!*

As the broadcast unfolded, the discussion in the chat became sharper. Jason's defenders clashed with those demanding he should be locked up again, debating the authenticity of Anita's letter and the implications for the first trial.

But Emma stuck with it. She thought she was right. She wanted the truth, whatever that would mean. She wanted justice, whatever that would cost. Her voice was huskier at the end of the letter. More purposeful.

"You can't know this and not act upon what you know. You can't let this lie. Jason White has to answer for this. He has to pay for what he has done," she concluded.

A final flurry of activity erupted as soon as she logged off. Some fans swore they would stick by Jason, believing he was innocent until the police proved otherwise. Others admonished the authorities for their failure to arrest and ostracise him again swiftly.

But for Emma, the answer was clear: she'd launched a series of events that would again thrust Jason's case into the national light and force him to reckon with who he was and the cost of his liberty. And as she sat back from the camera, exhausted yet grimly determined, she wasn't convinced that justice was done. However, her media popularity was back, and her bank account was as it had never been before.

Texts were flying back and forth on social media as followers tried to make sense of the bombshell evidence about how they were so shocked that Anita lied on the stand – and how her lies took Jason out of prison, tarnishing her mother's memory.

Soon, the story picked up steam and was circulated like a press release across news websites and online forums. *Miscarriage of justice! Rotten judges! Heartless betrayal! The terrible, terrible White family*. It was the case that the whole nation had been watching five years before. But now it was back in the news and stayed there for days.

But amid all that, Michael Jones was confronted by the urgent reality that Jason, who'd just gone away on a brief holiday abroad, needed to come home now. The lawyer was getting bad vibes, a deep-seated, sick, clawing pit in his stomach: he'd done his best to bury the truth for so long, and now it was about to explode into three separate lives, and it would be devastating.

Yet he began to realise he had let an innocent man go to prison, all the guilt about this burden he carried with him for so many years coming to a head, and now, due to his cowardice and ill judgment, an innocent man would be sent back to prison for at least another five years without a chance of parole, because of him.

However, as a lawyer, he also knew that everything he had done would bore into his bones like a guilty conscience, exposing him to sanctions by the Bar Association or even criminal charges. The idea of having his licence taken away, let alone the cataclysmic reputation he faced by betraying his client and the court system, squeezed him into dry sweatpants. He felt himself drowning. The clamour of warning bells had gone off in his ears.

Beyond the professional consequences, there was the unrelenting personal price exacted by his choices. He had allowed Jason, the 20-year-old man he'd 'sworn to defend, protect and promote all the rights which are secure by the laws of this country, so help me God', to be condemned to the life of horror that he had endured sitting in prison for eight years for a crime he hadn't committed. His violation of the principles of his profession was a breach of sentiment no lesser than the betrayal he would have committed had he endorsed Germaine's crimes by validating what she'd done in the name of justice. This was what kept Michael up at night. The guilt would never subside.

Meanwhile, as the media storm raged, Jamal was the first to start banging away at Emma's side, suggesting that she was exploiting the situation to line her pockets. In a shopping list of increasingly disgusted posts and videos, he claimed that her latest revelation regarding her OnlyFans was more evidence of a person who wouldn't stop until she had ruined someone's reputation and life. All of a sudden, Jamal found himself to side Jason.

His frenzy peaked as he accused Emma of another *treachery, a ruthless, hungry snake* intent on *selling out whoever she met*, driven by *vanity and greed*. His words were met with rousing applause, cheers coming from those already long in suspicion of Emma. Anger and condemnation rose to a keening pitch.

Just as she was moving from place to place to hide, the police showed up at her door with a warrant to see the letter as evidence in the reopened case. She went, all of a sudden, on a Live feed on Instagram: "It's the one time I almost lost my shit online," she admitted referring to something only she could understand. "They asked me to give them the letter so they could enter it into evidence. All of a sudden, it was real."

Suddenly, she was giving the Police the letter feeling this rising panic start to catch up with her. Like the rush of the exposé, the excitement of being the centre of the whirlwind, it began to go to something different inside, pinch in on her, and start making her feel uneasy about her actual reasons behind doing it.

The allure of wreaking vengeance helped her through the following dark days.

Jason, meanwhile, continued to enjoy the sunshiny beaches in Andalusia, largely oblivious to what was going on back home. He had a little more than a day to spend there before he could fly back to the UK, but he was free and loving life for the first time in a long time.

Michael couldn't look away from the consequences of his actions. They consumed his every waking moment. It was a fear of a devastating reckoning that he had been dreading for years, descending on him in real-time: the dirt would get turned over, the fruit would fall, and the tree's roots would finally be exposed for what they were. When the reckoning comes – when you're forced to reckon, you might say – you come face-to-face with the man who looks back at you: who you've become, the choices that got you there, and the part of you that knows in advance that you're going to pay.

## *31. The Arrest*

The world turned upside down when he got off the plane. That's when his life changed. Again. Jason was still reeling from the week he'd just experienced, having flown into Gatwick Airport on a Sunday night from a Cadiz-based holiday destination known as Viva La Vida when a unit of police intercepted him and asked if he would follow them to a police room there at the airport "concerning the manslaughter" of his father, Harry White. "We can't stay here overnight," they added, so "it would be advisable you contact your lawyer before we start even talking about the matter."

The officers stared at Jason with faces he couldn't read. They did not explain but quietly hinted at him to use the phone to call his lawyer. His fingers were shaking as they held the telephone to his ear. He dialled the number for Michael—his friend, attorney, and godfather. He waited. His heart was hammering.

Michael's voice was tight with apology. "Jason, I'm so sorry all of this happened. I've already asked my colleague, Josh Silverman, to go to Gatwick. He'll be there shortly to represent you."

If he didn't know any better, it might have seemed that Michael's words were confusing him on purpose. "Wait," he sputtered. "Your lawyer? Why can't you be? Michael... What's going on?"

There was a long silence on the phone line before Michael continued sombrely: "I can't represent you on this matter, Jason. There is a conflict involving me in these new allegations. I'm sorry, but I must withdraw from your case."

The world turned on itself around Jason as he tried to reconcile the situation. What were these new allegations that Michael was talking about? Why was his most trusted ally deserting him in his hour of need? Left bewildered and hanging, he looked at the police and staggered the now-familiar words: "Sir, I don't know. I'd like to know – why I'm here?" His voice broke as tears escaped from his eyes.

The officers looked at each other, and one of them took command. "Mr White, we can tell this is a strange and confusing time for you, but we think it's best to wait for your lawyer to get here before we get into the details. We know this is hard, but we'd appreciate it if you'd just be patient."

Helplessness washed over him as he fell back onto a chair nearby. Theories and possibilities crowded his mind, each worse than the one before. Was new evidence uncovered that pinned the murder on him? Had the verdict been false? Was someone now presenting false evidence to ensure he would return to jail? Emma? Jamal? Anita?

He could feel the weight of this uncertainty pulling at him like a heavy mass, and as hot tears rolled down his cheeks, he sobbed uncontrollably in his seat. Shaking, his body pressed against the chair, trying to keep himself together, while he realised that this nightmare was far from over, that even the future he had let himself hope for might be compromised yet again.

In that dark, windowless and impersonal room at Gatwick Airport now, with the police looking on impassively, his lawyer still on his way, he could do nothing for the moment but wait and pray that some god or selfhood would enable him to weather what was coming. But then again, given his past, had he ever been free from real ghosts? Nothing was ever done with the dead. His Dad was haunting him. 'Fuck him! Fuck the bastard,' he thought.

## *32. Anita*

Anita White (now Anita Trelawney) settled down as far as possible. She moved to the seaside town of St Ives in Cornwall, where she met her husband, Glenn, and her first son, Henry, was born only a year earlier. Here, thanks to a hefty inheritance, she opened a small souvenir shop and concentrated, happily, on domestic life. Time passed, and the painful memories of Jason faded away. It was not a wrong way to escape.

However, that day, when the police entered her shop, Anita felt the backlash of her past engulf her again. "And they came in, holding their heads down, and they asked me to close the shop for a while," she said out loud when the police entered, her heart fluttering. She complied.

When the police took out a copy of her letter for her to see, time began to stand still. She looked at the writing in front of her – her writing – as if the ghost of Anita years earlier had met the living version. "Mrs Trelawney," the officer asked softly, "do you recognise that letter? Was it your handwriting in the letter that was sent?"

Her voice trembled as she replied, "Yes, I wrote it. It's authentic."

The officer nodded. "You're charged Mrs Trelawney with perjury in court and perverting the course of justice. Come with us."

Her limbs seemed to give way. Her head was spinning. She thought of her husband, two hours away at work, her son, and the life she'd fought for. "Can I call my husband?" she asked, swelling with rage, her voice little more than a whisper. "He needs to know what's going on."

The officer nodded and gave her the phone. She dialled Glenn's number, and when he picked up, she found it hard to suppress her sadness.

"Glenn? It's me. Something's happened. I … I might not be coming home for a while. I need you to look after Henry for me."

Glenn's voice was puzzled and worried. "Anita, what's happening? Are you Okay?"

Tears coursed down her cheeks as she struggled to speak. "It's about me. About my past. My family. I… I can't explain everything now, but I need you to stick by Henry. For us. I love you."

He stood quietly momentarily, and she imagined him trying to take the information in. "I love you too, Annie. Whatever this is, we'll be Okay, I promise. I am coming back home to pick Henry up from the childminder."

When Anita returned the telephone, she felt a chill of fear and remorse. Hadn't she thought that at last, she had vanquished the ghosts of her past, that she had come to terms with the horror that had torn her family apart? Now a mother and owner of a little shop in St Ives, surrounded by police disrupting the peace of this sunny resort town in south-west England, hadn't she opened the ghastly doorway again by taking the law into her own hands?

Years earlier, on the 15th of October, some decisions had sent ripples through the White family that were still simmering to the boil. And even though she'd feared it, she realised she couldn't elude them forever. She finally had to face them, no matter how terrible the reckoning.

With her escape to Cornwall, away from the house where it all began, she sensed a grim determination to see it through, to bear whatever came from it. She had fought to create a life and a loving, stable family, to put events of the past behind her; now, she would have to summon that same steel to face the darkest part of her history, the last time in which the ghosts of that place – those awful ghosts – might come back. For her and her family, for her brother 'whom I betrayed in the pursuit of peace for all of us'.

## *33. Josh*

Josh Silverman strode through the doorway to the passenger waiting area at Gatwick Airport like a high-voltage hurricane. A short, compact man around 50, he had a wild mound of salt-and-pepper hair and beard and a suit – if that's what it was – consisting of a rumpled raincoat and a discoloured tie hanging over barely long enough trousers, which were topped by mismatched socks and scuffed shoes.

But as messy as he was, Josh's eyes were intelligent, just a glimpse of something profound in the clumsy exterior. He scanned the room and noted the fellow on the chair with Jason looking so sad in the corner, surrounded by a few fat cops.

"All right, all right, all right," a booming Geordie voice said. "Blimey, if it isn't the Jason White! Been a long time, old man!"

Jason looked up, saucer eyes. "I'm sorry," he muffled, "You must have confused me with someone else."

Josh broke out laughing and sat down beside him in the chair. "I guess not, but I'd known you anyway." "Really?" was Jason's response. "Yeah, man. Michael told me all about you."

Jason nodded unsurely, still reeling from a cyclone of a man who had just appeared in the room.

The lawyer, at least Jason assumed he was, despite his look, leant in toward his client conspiratorially, his eyebrows waggling. "Three hours they've got you locked up in here? Blimey! Has Dey been treating you well? Dey feed ya? C'mon, I tell you, have you ever tasted airport food? Aeroplane food ah ah ahh, that's bad enough, but airport holden food de zee is cruel, unusual, and criminal, pardon the pun!"

Not that Jason could muster up much of a smile, given the moment's gravity, but Josh's irreverence did bring a slight smirk to his face. "No, no food. Just a lot of waiting and wondering."

Josh fixed his eyes on the policewoman in the room. 'Wot about you, love,' he said, his tone conspiratorial. 'Parading your nightstick and handcuffs up and down our jails. You have been trying to climb into this lady's pants, Miss Plod, 'cause there are easier ways, believe me, to make a date than arresting a bloke!'

The policewoman glared at Josh, who grinned back at her, unfazed. On the other hand, Jason was doing his best to conceal a laugh at the lunacy of his lawyer's remarks.

Josh looked back at Jason. His expression was now serious. "But seriously, boy, what's going on here? Michael calls me in a flat panic, saying you need a lawyer yesterday, some BS. What did you do this time?"

Jason shook his head. He had been amused for a moment, but now his cheerfulness slipped away. "I don't know. I just got off the plane, and these officers come up to me, saying something about my Dad's manslaughter... But I thought that was all, that I'd been cleared of all this."

Josh grimaced, and then he nodded. "OK, never mind, let's see if we can get to the bottom of this. Um, officers?" He said grandly to the police, holding his arms, "Can you help us and explain why my client is detained? Don't try and scrimp on the detail, please – we've got all the time in the world... at least until the pub shuts and I miss out on a pint."

The officers began to tell their side of the story, and Josh started listening. His joking attitude vanished; he looked at Jason with his full attention. He looked back and could only wait on the side, his chest tight and heart pounding as he wondered: 'How did I get back here so soon?'

The policeman coughed into his fist to grab Jason's attention, deep in his thoughts, and his eyes were sad as he spoke to him. "Mr White," he said. "We've got new evidence that contradicts what your sister claimed about your mother's killing your father in your trial. Recently, we received a letter written by Anita White that addressed you. In the letter, your sister says she lied on the stand about your mother's involvement in your father's death."

Jason's eyes bulged, his mouth flapping soundlessly as he tried to respond. "I – I can't deny she wrote that letter. But you have to consider – my mother told me on one of her visits to me in jail that she did it. Anita didn't believe me when I told her, but I think she started to have misgivings in the end, and that's why she came round."

"Hey, dude, dude – whoa there, now. Don't go spouting all the details. You got to follow my advice, Jason. I can tell you're excited to give a blow-by-blow, but for now, I'd appreciate it if you stay mum about this." Josh put a hand on Jason's shoulder. "I got this one, alright?"

The young man just nodded. He was looking at Josh with a bewildered frown. He folded his arms across his chest and sat back down.

"Officer," Josh said, turning to the policeman, "my client has gone through a lot. There are still a lot of questions that need answering. Why don't we continue this conversation another time when I've had a chance to review the evidence and chat with my client in private?"

The policeman nodded and did not for a moment remove his expressionless stare from Silverman's face. "All right then, Mr Silverman," he clarified. "I'm now going to have to tell you that, given this new information, we have no choice but to book Mr White and put him in a holding cell at a local prison, pending a new trial."

Josh's face lit up, the corners of his mouth curling upwards, his blue eyes glinting underneath furrowed brows. "Local prison, you say?" he said. "And I don't suppose you could send him to Brixton either, could you? I've just heard they've opened a cocktail bar down there, and I'd love to check it out, given all the time I will spend with my client!"

The policewoman had been silent during the discussion, but now she said: "Brixton? I'm afraid that's out of the question, Mr

Silverman. But Inverness, maybe. I hear that the prison has a grand view of the countryside."

Josh held his heart in pretend agony. "Inverness? You wound me, Constable. And I thought we were getting along like the Duke and Duchess of Cambridge."

For all the moment's seriousness, Jason smiled slightly as his lawyer and the policewoman exchanged their clash of words. A moment of humour before the seriousness, perhaps.

But as the police officers prepared to escort Jason to jail, Josh moved in close, his tone soft and soothing. "Don't worry, mate. We'll get to the bottom of this. I'm here to make sure it's upright in the end, you know? Even if I have to apply a little pressure. And then, when the truth comes out, you'll have a roof over your head, and we'll see about that cocktail bar. Not necessarily in that order."

Jason nodded. Hope smiled slightly as two figures in plain clothes led him away, even if it were in a prison with a view.

But now, with all he had been through, he could look at the door and feel better because he had Josh with him. He might be able to face whatever they were about to tell him with something akin to humour and certainly with a lot of Geordie.

## 34. Jamal

Since Jason's release from prison, Jamal's life had gone into a downward spiral as he remained engrossed in his obsessive thoughts about the man who'd taken over his life. It had taken a considerable toll on him: he became mildly aggressive and unable to mix with people or build close relationships. Instead, he was a recluse, spending all his days and nights in his bedsit. His fantasies were all about Jason. No other man would have been good enough.

He could relieve his sexual urges more times a day, just remembering the last time they met.

He'd dropped out of university, his promising student career scuppered by the relentlessness of his obsession. Now, he was working part-time as a waiter in a bar in Bedford—nothing like the plans he must have had for himself. The only relief from the numbing repetitiveness of his days came from the endless whirring of his brain, which kept returning to Jason and the wrongs done to him.

He had gone down the rabbit hole of hybristophilia, spending countless hours online reading about it, learning more about his obsession, and communicating with other hybristophiles. But he had no idea it was a paraphilia, believing his feelings for Jason were true love rather than a mental illness.

The rejection and the knowledge that Emma had scooped him up started eating away at him like a toxic acid. He put all his energy into proving what he increasingly believed was her duplicitous and selfish behaviour – in his mind, particularly concerning the money she had raised through her online crowdsourcing campaigns. He was sure she had stolen the money for herself and wanted everyone else to see it, too. He was determined to destroy her.

Yet none of this did any good to his cause. He was still unravelling, unable to make any noteworthy progress against Emma's influence—the more he complained and tried to shame her in public, the more ignored, isolated, and powerless he felt.

As he traversed the next few years, life after life, he realised that in losing himself in obsession for Jason, he had lost himself altogether. Completely. The brilliant younger version of himself became someone else entirely, someone he no longer fully recognised as he hid under the guise of the man luring a lover who knew not what lured him.

Nevertheless, in his most desperate moments, he still insisted that his love for Jason was the one worthwhile, pure thing he had in his life. He told himself that if he could hold out, hold on, and believe hard enough, he'd eventually force Jason to see him and learn to return his affection.

This delusion kept him grinding his pained bones along sad alleyways, yet it was also the island of sanity he could wisp back to when a world that had increasingly seemed foreign to him turned to waves of fire, chips of rain, and hands of ice. He ploughed on, his heart drawing him ever closer to the man who was a bridge to the life he was being deprived of and a reservoir for the misery that was destroying the life he had.

The news of Anita's letter and its stunning contents brought the powder keg he carried around inside him back to the boil. He became galvanised to show that he could help Jason, redeeming his lack of action. In the ensuing days, he got back in the swing of spreading the word and campaigning for Jason's release.

Desperate to reach out to the object to his infatuation, he emailed him directly, sending him a series of broken-hearted emails in which he voiced his feelings and vowed to be true. He was convinced that this time, Jason would see him for who he indeed was and return his feelings in kind. Jason didn't see his email, as he had no access to the external world in prison. Jamal knew that, but he would not give up, and he started writing letters.

## *35. Michael*

Michael was in the office in East London when he met Josh.

The office felt dark and cramped; something was wrong with the air. His breath caught in his throat. "Josh, it's about me," he said and paused. "I did something bad. I went back, and I changed it."

His voice cracked. "I have something to say about the previous trials. Something I kept secret too long."

Leaning forward, his face creased with worry: "Mate, come to big brother. Whatever it is that is on your mind, you can tell me."

Michael looked up, his hands clasped together in front of him. "Before the first trial, Germaine told me that she did kill Harry…" He continued with his narration while his words hung over theoffice like a blanket of suffocation. Josh took a step back and sat in a chair.

"Jesus, Michael," he breathed. "That's a hell of a secret to keep. Now I understand why you asked me to take over from you."

Michael ran his hands over his face again with the same haunted look. "I knew. And then, when the verdict came back when they sentenced him to eight years in prison, I knew that I'd done something wrong…"

While Michael was discussing the ordeal, Josh looked at his colleague and nodded, processing what he heard. "If this comes out, Michael, you realise that means disbarment, the end of your career, and possible criminal charges."

Michael's shoulders sagged beneath the weight of what he had done. "I know. But I can't live with it anymore. He's paying for my mistakes. For the mistakes of a friend."

Silverman leaned in. "Michael," he whispered urgently, "you can't ever tell anyone this, you understand? Not Jason, not anyone. Not even to the court. If anyone asks, you say that Germaine told you before the appeal during one of those appointments you had written in your agenda… You can't ever contradict that. You got it?"

Michael shook his head. "That's the thing. After that first trial, Germaine never scheduled another appointment. I couldn't look at her again."

The two men sat for a long moment, their joint knowledge biting smoky air between them. Finally, Josh spoke.

"There's something I don't get. How did Emma get that letter from Anita? The one that blew the whole thing wide open again?"

Michael's eyebrows disappeared in a V of concern. "I don't know, mate. I didn't even know about the content of that letter. If I had known, I would have told Jason to rip it to shreds. Damn, kid!"

Josh's nod was grim. "Between us, we must figure out what Emma's doing. What can be her game in sending that letter now, and what she intends."

Michael gave a deflated sigh. 'She is a manipulative bitch. She got me to write a letter to justify her use of funds she raised to run the Free Jason campaign. She is a cunt. She is a scorned woman who can't accept that Jason wants to bury his past. You hear about hybristophilia, right?" Josh nodded. "She's the quintessence of it. Once the hero is no longer a hero, she feels betrayed and would do anything to destroy him. Poor guy..."

Josh shook his head. "Ok. So there is not much we can do so far. The wheels of justice grind exceedingly slowly. But I will see Anita soon – she's in a prison in South West England. HMP Eastwood Park, as far as I know. Maybe she might tell us something. The poor girl is going to be trialled, too, for perjury. It's incredible how families can destroy people."

Michael's eyes opened more expansive, and their colour showed a trace of optimism. "Yeah, maybe she can tell more. It would be good. Maybe she'll shed some light."

Then, he leaned back in his chair and smiled. "And what about our boy Jason, eh? I can't imagine how this has been for him, putting him back into the lion's den, eh?"

"He's doing just fine, man, as good as possible. He's a tough kid. He's been through hell and back," Josh said gently, with a hint of pride in his voice. Michael continued, "It's made him stronger. Nothing like I'd thought it would. He ain't the same scared, little shitheel who tried to move to Cape North that bloody night. He's a man. A survivor."

Josh nodded, and Michael could see admiration in Josh's eyes.

The two men were quiet for a minute, mulling their responsibilities, hopes, and apprehensions regarding the road ahead.

## 36. *The Reactions*

The publication of Anita's letter and Jason White's arrest the following week propelled the case into the national spotlight. They set off a frenzy of media commentary and social-media speculation.

Within hours of the announcement, *#JasonWhiteTrial* was trending on Twitter, with thousands of users tweeting their opinions on this latest twist in the story. Many expressed outrage at the notion a guilty man could have been released, sending messages that he must receive the harshest punishment and calling for justice to be served as quickly as possible.

*Domestic assault survivors shake their heads, nod in recognition, and breathe a sigh of relief; that can never be the end of what Jason White did to his father. If Jason White did kill his Dad, he needs to pay for it,* one Tweeter wrote. *No years in prison can bring back the life he destroyed.*

But other experts took Jason's side, noting the whole life of abuse that he had suffered from his father and the lifelong trauma.

*We cannot ignore the context of Jason's actions here either. He was a victim of severe abuse, and traumatic abuse does not just disappear overnight. He needs help, not more jail time.*

In the meantime, Chiswick was entirely off the map as the Whites were no longer members of their community. The residents kept enjoying their Sunday market, their High Road walks, and their enviable lifestyle.

*Anita was excellent throughout the whole process. I loved the way she stood by Jason. She went through unbelievable hell to keep her brother free and has stuck by him through thick and thin. I love you so much, Anita.*

One commenter wrote that Anita lied to keep her brother out of prison. *Loyalty, love, and support are things that every family should have.*

While she remained in jail, waiting for her trial, others began to speak out against her, accused of perverting justice and turning the state against itself.

*Anita White is just as guilty as her brother,* one other user posted. *She lied under oath, which is also a crime! Kick her white ass in prison.*

If the coverage was initially confined to social media, the mainstream Press joined the fray, editorialists and legal commentators rushing to offer their views as the storm gained intensity.

Saying the case had been reopened, defenders of Jason and his family—on the morning talk shows, among other places—paraded criminal defence attorneys and former prosecutors who told the country that Anita's letter was grounds for a complete dismissal of the charges against Jason as in that letter, there was no clear proof that what she wrote was the truth.

"This case was tainted from the start," one TV pundit claimed. "Evidences were ignored. No social services were involved, and no testimony was used to release the man, violating the most basic tenets of Jason's rights. He should get a new trial but be acquitted."

However, others protested that the evidence against Jason was still too strong and that a retrial was the only way they could be sure that justice had been served.

"But look. Is there any doubt that the reason for that senior person's death was his son, Jason White? Intentional or not, death occurred because of him, the son, and the only way to punish him is to retry him."

While legal manoeuvres were playing out, the court finally decided that Jason White would have a new trial, but house arrest was denied. The date for that retrial was just a month away, and the court members and the general public alike would be left reeling.

The news validated Emma's move to publish Anita's letter, proof that she had been right to advocate for the truth at any cost. It also gave Jamal a bitter pill to swallow, a reminder of what he considered a gross injustice served upon his friend Jason—and the long road yet to clear his name and restore his reputation.

The media show intensified in the weeks before the start of the new trial, as reporters pitched tents on the courthouse steps and pundits predicted the case's outcome.

Jason knew that he was on the side of the right, and with that confidence, he would have walked into the courtroom.

## 37. *Anita*

Josh arrived at HMP Eastwood Park, a women's prison in the wooded middle of Gloucestershire, like an unexpected visit from a past he had gotten too acquainted with due to his profession. The red brick building loomed grimly against the landscape, cut off from the outside world by a looming perimeter of fences.

But the footfall of Josh Silverman, who was making his way down one of the blinds to speak to Anita, echoed as if off shellac. 'It's another of those places that you can visit only once, having heard enough about how people behave in conditions such as these not to want to return.'

Following a search of his person and a thorough pat-down, he was escorted to the prison visiting room, a practical space with a few half-dozen tables and chairs welded to the floor. Across from him was her, jaundiced from fluorescent light, sightless eyes. Anita looked old, lines canvassing her once sculpted features, unyielding and shrivelled.

"Call me Josh," he said softly and slowly, moving to his seat opposite her. "Thank you for being here."

Anita looked up, met his eyes briefly, and then darted away. "I didn't have a say, after all," she whispered. "Not after what I've done."

He leaned across the table, elbows resting, and fixed his gaze on her face. "It's hard for you."

It was deeply uncomfortable for both, but Josh wanted her to get to the bottom of her feelings.

He cocked his head and lowered his voice. "Why the letter? Help me understand."

For some time, she didn't reply; her fingers fidgeted anxiously on her lap. "I didn't mean to do it to hurt Jason," she said, eyes filling with tears. "I thought I was doing the right thing – I wanted him to know how I felt about the whole thing. But instead, I've just made things worse."

The lawyer nodded. "I know. But Anita. Did you lie on the stand during the appeal?"

She turned her head around, her eyes widening with fear. "No!" she said, her voice high-pitched. "No, I didn't lie. I did think that my mum had killed my Dad. That's what I told the court."

His forehead knotted. "But your letter... So why'd you write it if you thought it was true?"

Her lower lip started quivering, and for a moment, Josh thought she would cry. "I don't know," she replied in a whisper. "I was so messed up, so scared. I didn't want to believe that my mum had done this, that Jason was telling the truth. Mum had just died, and I felt like I needed to do something for her, to protect her memory, but at the same time, I didn't want everyone to know the truth..."

"Anita, I just told you, it's a fact. I know, but..." he sighed. "But, honey. You don't understand."

"I don't?" she sounded perplexed.

"You don't understand the consequences of your actions?" continued Josh.

"What consequences? My letter didn't hurt or harm anyone, at least Jason."

Josh was astonished by this statement.

Her head fell, her shoulders shaking with silent sobs. "I know," she whispered. "I know. And I'm so, so sorry. I never wanted any of this."

Josh put his hand on the table, palm up, and slowly reached across it and put his hand on Anita's arm. He said softly: "I know you didn't, but we're in this mess now. I need you to be honest with me, sweetheart. I can get Jason out of it."

Then she looked up; her eyes were bloodshot, her lids inflamed. "What do you want me to do?" she said tremblingly.

Josh's expression was severe, but his eyes were compassionate. "I want you to tell the truth," he said. "I want you to testify at Jason's retrial, in court, and tell what happened. It won't be easy. It'll not be easy. But it's the only way Jason will get the justice he needs. I want you to recall anything from your youth years. Everything about your family life and everything that can confirm what you, as a child, had to go through. We need to prove that your mother had a serious motive to wish her husband dead. Yes, social services have already proven that, but the jury might be more, how do you say, softened if it comes from a child of the victim."

She didn't speak for a long time. Her eyes were far away and unfocused. Then she slowly nodded. Her shoulders straightened, and a look of resolution touched her eyes.

"Right," she whispered. "I'll tell them. I'll tell them everything. Let them kill me if they want."

Josh smiled, feeling his chest swell with pride. "Thank you," he said, the words catching in his throat. "It's not easy, of course – but you're doing the right thing. And I don't want you to ever worry about that. The truth will get out, Jason will not be punished for what he hasn't done, and your mum will get all the sympathy she needed when she was in life because she was the victim of this story..." He didn't continue his sentence, but he implied 'instead of your Dad'.

Those few words released him from his chair, and he took time, before he touched the guard on the shoulder, to squeeze Anita's arm gently with his hand. Then he hoisted himself up, nodded goodbye, and walked out of the prison, already planning what needed to be done to try the case.

His walk into the bright sunlight of the prison yard renewed that tantalisingly small burst of hope that had been virtually snuffed out in the few months after Jason's conviction.

## 38. Jamal and Josh

It was hard to imagine a chapter of this meaningful tale being written down a quiet side street in Putnoe, a suburb of Bedford. But there was Josh Silverman, sitting opposite Jamal Adams, a man who had become known as one of Jason White's most devoted fanatics.

"Thank you for seeing me here in Bedford, Mr Silverman," Jamal said gravely. "I know you're a very busy man. But these days I cannot afford to leave the town and visit you in London. But at the same time, I didn't want to miss this chance."

Josh nodded in acknowledgement; his face impassive as he scrutinised the man before him. "Well, okay, Jamal. I'm always glad to talk to someone who cares as much about Jason as you do. But to be candid, I'm missing something... I don't understand why you wanted to talk to me."

Jamal's lips curled into a smile, but no humour was in his eyes. "It's Emma. Like I said many times, she's been spreading lies about Jason, setting him up to look like a monster. But I'm telling you, he's not a monster. Jason, you can see that yourself, so why are people listening to Emma? She's the monster."

Josh's eyebrows went up. "What do you mean?" he asked, his pen still over his notepad.

Jamal pulled his chair back and tapped his long fingers on the table's edge. "You want to know the truth?" he asked in his low, intimate voice. "I did my homework. Emma has been skimming money from Jason White's defence fund, taking money that belongs to the cause and pocketing it for herself. She's been parading around like she's Mother Theresa, but she's nothing but a whoreson bitch."

Josh's eyes widened. What he was hearing was no news as he had was aware of the smearing campaign online, however, he sensed that there was more to come. "What are you talking about, Jamal?" he questioned slowly. "That's a big accusation. Do you have evidence?"

Jamal's grin widened as he leaned forward, reaching into his breast pocket. He pulled out a slim folder. "Here you go," he said, pushing the folder across the table. "Bank statements, emails, all the evidence. Emma has been siphoning cash off Jason's supporters for months and using the money for her inflated lifestyle. At the same time, she's been doing her best to destroy Jason's reputation, smearing him and claiming he's a sexual predator. All because she's insane, plain as that – obsessed with Jason."

Josh frowned, skimming the pages. "Obsession?" he said. "You know, obsess ... about ..." He searched the air.

A shadow fell over Jamal's face, his eyes narrowing as he leaned closer, his voice a low, menacing growl. "Emma is fucked-up, simple as that. She has a condition called hybristophilia. She's into crime, into guys who've done bad things. She's been in love with Jason for years, ever since he got first nicked. And now she's trying to ruin him because he dumped her."

That thought ping-ponged around Josh's brain. It was not that he cared about the paraphilia, as he knew Jamal was equally affected by it. Something else was tickling his curiosity. How did he get Emma's statements? He thought it was better not to ask.

"And you, Jamal? And why precisely do you care about Jason's case?"

There was a beat of silence, and then Jamal looked up and met his eyes. "I love him," he said in a soft voice. He repeated it. "I'll never deny who he is. I can acknowledge what he's done. But above all of that, I love him. This may sound crazy, but I've loved Jason since I first saw him. I don't look at him as just some criminal. I see a human being. He's a gorgeous, messed-up little fuck who needs someone to believe in him."

As Josh's hand settled on Jamal's arm, he softly said, "I get it." His throat momentarily constricted from emotion. I will do everything I can so the truth comes out, and Jason can live his life."

Jamal lifted his gaze, his brown eyes brilliant with unshed tears. "I can't thank you enough," he gasped, his voice half-lost in the clatter and chatter. "Thank you for believing in him and for fighting for him. I know it will be difficult, but I also know that you are on his side; Jason has a chance."

Josh smiled. Knowing that he got up, letting his hand rest on Jamal's arm a little longer than usual before he turned and left the café, his mind already turning, the work on the case beginning.

As he committed to the bright sunlight of the Bedford suburb, he felt the truth would come out.

## 39. *Michael and Josh*

As Josh and Michael sat across from each other in Michael's office – a large, book-lined room that betrayed the elite status of the large firm that had nurtured Michael's career over the past two decades – the only outward manifestation of either man's angst was a faint blue pall that cloaked their attentive, pinched faces.

Josh leant forward in his chair, elbows on the desk, fixing Michael with a piercing stare: "Michael, about what you said. About the fee you got for defending Jason."

"What about it?" Michael sat back and folded his hands across his lap. His brow had become furrowed.

Josh sighed, his fingertips drumming a crackling beat on the desktop. "I've spoken to Jamal and have some questions for you. He's suspicious of Emma; he thinks she's been misappropriating funds from any money she's raised for Jason's defence and using it for herself. Somehow, he managed to get hold of Emma's bank and credit card statements for the last few years – don't ask me how – and I see no professional fees paid for you, and I do not see any massive cash withdrawal to pay your fees."

At this, Michael's face darkened, and he leaned in a little toward Josh, his voice sounding almost like a confession spoken quietly by a penitent. "I know," he said. "But I didn't want to say anything because I felt it might hurt his case."

Josh's eyes widened. He reeled back in his chair. "What?" he said. His voice was already tight.

Michael sighed, and his shoulders seemed to droop under the weight of it all. "I just ... I didn't get the fees. I told them I got them to keep it out of the news so that Jason wouldn't be harassed over this mess about the defence fund. I never told a lie before, but I told that one to protect him."

For the longest time, Josh didn't say anything. "I understand why you did it," he said slowly, looking up from his plate. "You wanted to save Jason, protect him from the world. But, mate, what you just did is wrong. It's unethical. It was a lie, and there might be consequences for that behaviour. It seems like you have been looking for trouble all the way."

Michael nodded, his face grim. "I know." His voice was a little louder than a whisper. "And I'm sorry. I never meant it to go this far, but I couldn't stand by as she pulled Jason apart, destroying him and his chance to grow into a better man."

Leaning in, Josh lowered his voice. "I'm telling you, she has used the money for herself. But we have to be prudent about this. We can't come out guns blazing accusing Emma of embezzlement when we can't prove it – we could also end up hurting Jason."

"You're right; she's done nothing against the law. As much as I hate to say it, I don't think what Emma did is criminal. Her doing, what she did was unethical. She was wrong to do it. But ethically... And legally... It's not enough to press charges to make her pay the price."

For a long time, Josh stayed in a deliberate silence. Then his face cleared, and he sat up in his chair. "Maybe not," he said. "But you'd scare her, you think? Make her think about things?" and looking at the ceiling, with his index finger tapping his chin... "I suppose I'd scare her."

Michael's brows lifted, and he leaned forward, his eyes twinkling. "What do you mean?" asked, his voice a conspiratorial whisper.

Josh smiled slowly, a predatory grin that lit up his face. "I think we should ask the court to grant us access to Emma's accounts," he replied. "All of them, and the full details of every penny she's raised and spent on Jason's behalf. But there's no need to accuse her, not yet. The threat of exposure, of having the sordid details of her private life revealed in public, might persuade her to back off, to think about what she's doing."

There was a long pause before Michael spoke again. His eyebrows drew together solemnly, and then he slowly began to nod.

His smile spread. "That might work," he said, speaking more slowly and deliberately than usual. "It's a risk, but we must take it. For Jason. For the truth." And continued, "But you will never get it before the trial."

Josh nodded solemnly. "Right, we gotta do what we gotta do to give the boy a fair trial, to ensure he's not railroaded into another five years of hell. Play a little dirty? If that is what it takes, so be it. Oh, by the way, I do not need those statements, remember? I got them already, courtesy of Mr. Jamal Adams!"

## *40. Emma and Josh*

Josh Silverman tapped his desk with his fingers. The phone lay in front of him. He had a feeling the call he was about to make would tip the scales and might change what had seemed inevitable, even though it was a risk, ill-advised, a roll of the dice.

Sucking in a breath, he dialled the number for the lawyer assigned to look after Emma's affairs, Mary Saunders. The phone rang once, twice, three times before a calm, clear voice came on the line.

"This is Josh Silverman," came his calm, measured voice. "I'm representing Jason White, and I'm calling to ask if you and your client, Emma Wilkins, would be willing to have an off-the-record chat."

The lawyer made no reply for a moment. "I see," she said. "And er – what is this conversation about?"

Josh was leaning forward, elbows slipping through a taunt grip on the desk. "I have a piece of information that I would like to share with you and your client before the trial. I believe that it is information she would like to know. I believe it can potentially alter the trial's outcome and her reputation."

There was another long pause, and then the lawyer spoke – more grown-up this time. "Okay," she muffled, her voice tight with tension. "Let's meet, off the record. But only if you promise what we say can stay private."

"Would you like," asked Josh slowly, a terrible smile spreading across his face, "a drink?"

Two hours later, he sat across the desk from Emma and her attorney. Emma had been staying in North London during her new campaign, and with the support of her OnlyFans channel, she was making a hell of a living in London. She looked clenched and nervous. She was almost fidgeting, with her hands folded nervously in front of her, and she refused eye contact with Josh.

"Thank you so much for agreeing to meet with me," he began, his voice carefully measured. "I know that this case has been tough for everyone. And I appreciate you taking the time to have this conversation."

Mary nodded. Her face was as closed as a door. "Well, Mr Silverman, snap to it, for Christ's sake. What information do you believe you possess?"

He grinned, keeping his eyes locked on Emma's. "I have received information that shows Emma didn't pay for Michael Jones to work on the case, to find out exactly how that money was used. I have evidence that *Ems* didn't use the money raised for Jason's defence for that purpose."

Emma's eyes widened, and she sat straighter in her chair. "No!" she said. "That's not true. I paid Michael for his services. Why would I deny paying him?"

Josh shook his head, the pity in his expression light and mocking. "Unfortunately, no," he said. "I have bank statements. I have the accounts, and they prove that the girl spent the money raised on her existence. Emma, the showgirl. She went on holiday and bought her dog clothes, jewellery, and treats. A few hundred pounds here and there for some ad campaigns, but most of the money just on herself."

Mary's eyes welled up. "Even so," she said, her tone sober, "it is not illegal. Nothing in the law stops Emma from using the money for herself."

Josh blew out a breath through his lips and nodded. "You do raise some questions. Don't you?" The nod came slowly, his jaw slackening slightly. "But I still think we're close to figuring it out; we have to consider the possibility that Emma has this powerful motivation to support Jason for reasons we don't have to worry so much about."

He leaned toward the young woman. "And then there's what happened to the money when Emma and Jason were together," he continued, his tone suddenly more rapid. "None of that money ever came from Emma. Emma's own money paid for none. All of it was paid for; all of it was spent from Jason's savings."

Emma's face blanched, and she averted her eyes, shame and regret writing large; her lawyer lowered herself into the chair and fixed Josh with an expression of terminal resignation.

"What do you want?" she asked, her voice tired and defeated.

Josh smiled triumphantly. "I want her to agree to certain terms," he said slowly. "I want her to agree that she will not accuse Jason of anything that has nothing to do with what was in the letter. And I'll keep quiet about her financial transactions."

Emma's lawyer nodded. "And if we don't agree?" She spoke tight with tension.

Josh's mouth curled up at the corner, and he sat back in his chair. He wore a vindicated smile. "Then I'll have to be the one to expose all this," he said, heavily and slowly. "Emma is finished. Emma is ruined. How do you say, Emma? Hashtag, bye-bye, Emma?"

Emma's face crumpled, and she hunched over in her seat, resting her head in her hands, crying softly. Her lawyer sat back, her head hanging, dejected.

"I agree", Emma replied.

"Great!" Josh shouted, banging both hands on the table before him and getting up.

"All right?" he said, and the meeting broke up. He had gambled with Emma's reputation and that of Michael as well.

## 41. Jason and Josh

Josh sank into the hard plastic seat. He stared at Jason's face, noting the new creases of worry and the dullness in eyes that had once glinted with lust for life. The drag of his circumstances had defeated the young man.

"Jason," he began. "I know this has been a living hell for you. But I want you to know we're making inroads. Day by day, step by step, we're building a defence."

Jason's eyes lifted to Josh's. Wary hope flickered in their depths. "Be honest, Josh. Do you think I have a chance? After everything that's happened?"

The lawyer tilted forward on the rough table edge, his forearms down like combat antennae. "I do believe that. I do. Many of the reasons I do this are because of the people behind you who are prepared to advance the truth."

Jason's jaw tightened as a shadow passed over his face. "Like Emma?" he laughed. "I heard how she's been twisting and profiting from the narrative. She's a new influencer!"

Josh sighed. "I know. There's no denying how furious and disappointed you might be." He shook his head. "But the truth is, we might be able to exploit that. If we can get across that she had a vested interest, we might be able to create some genuine doubts about her credibility as a witness."

Jason was quiet for a long moment, his fingers tapping a nervous rhythm on the table. "What about Anita?" he asked in a barely whispered voice. "Have you talked to her?"

"I have. She is faring well. She is married and has a son now." Jason let himself go with a big smile. "I'm an uncle!"

Josh continued, "And Jason, she's ready to testify. Not about what happened the night your father died, as she was not in the room, but about everything. The abuse. The fear. The control he had over all your lives."

Jason's eyes grew wild, mixed feelings across his face – surprise, relief, wariness. "She's going to do that. She will go up there and talk about what he did to us?"

"She... she is. Yes, she is," Josh answered. "She also knows she's got a fight on her hands. But she knows it's the fight for you, your family, and her. She wants people to know what you went through, mate. What you all went through."

Jason's eyes glistened with unspent tears. His Adam's apple jumped as he swallowed audibly. "I don't know what to say," he said hoarsely. "I never thought ... I mean, I always hoped, but ..."

Josh leaned across the table to put a hand on Jason's forearm. "I know, mate, I know. How could you not be excited as fuck about this?" and laughed. "I'd be excited to jerk off about it, that's for sure."

Jason looked at Josh, embarrassment written on his face.

"Anything else?"

"When you're back there on the stand," Silverman explained, "they're going to try to manipulate your words, to make you question yourself and your memories. They're going to drag your past into the courtroom with you and use it against you."

Jason's shoulders sagged. "Shit. I don't know. I don't know how I could—facing all that shit, having them grill me about every little mistake I ever made... for the third time."

"You will," said Josh firmly, squeezing Jason's arm. "You're a fighter, boy. You've fought all your life, and here you are. Up there, keep your eye on the truth. Don't let them turn it around and throw it in your face. Don't jump around and try to please them. Please give them your truth and give them the real you. Trust the jury to understand there's more to you than that."

Jason was quiet for a minute, then swallowed and looked away, staring out the window, his eyes going soft and his lips slightly pursed as he thought. Then a breath, a nod of his head, a spark of something in his eyes.

"Okay," his voice was stronger. "Okay, I'll do it. I'll tell the truth no matter what they do to me. Because I owe it to myself if nothing else, and I'm sure as shit owe it to every one of the people who's standing up for me."

There was a swelling in Josh's chest, and his forceful throat closed up as he took in the quiet courage he was seeing in the young man in front of him. "I'm proud of you, Jason, more than you know. Regardless of what comes out of that courtroom next week, I want you to remember you have people here for you. People who believe in you and who will keep fighting for you."

There was a comfortable silence, or maybe it wasn't silent, as their thoughts gathered for the battle. But for a second, Josh thought that things might work out - that, while it would not be an easy ride, there would be hope along the bumpy road ahead.

# Part 6 – The Retrial

## 42. Back to Court

On the day of the retrial, *déjà vu* was in the air. The sprawling neo-Gothic stone-and-steel courthouse was the same, as was the drama playing out inside it. Among those on both sides of that battle were the people whose lives had been forever altered by Jason White.

Outside, hundreds of reporters and spectators craned their necks up towards the courthouse steps. They gathered to soak up the drama, watch a spectacle, and get a glimpse of something people would later tell their children and grandchildren about. Friday afternoon's atmosphere was charged and explosive, a hum of voices overlaid with clicking cameras and scratchy pencil-to-pad sounds.

The electricity was charged in the courtroom, and the tinderbox was dense. The gallery was packed—old faces and unfamiliar ones—and the breath held tight. The wooden benches creaked under the weight of the silent bodies, sharing whispery streams of predatory chatter, their hum filling the room.

Seated at the defence table between his lawyer, Josh Silverman, and a large enrolment book, Jason looked like a choirboy who'd had a furious stare painted on his face. The Geordie sat stiff, his chin thrust out at an absurd angle. His hair was combed instead of sticking up in disarray; the suit was still brand-new, and the tie was knotted straight. It had all come down to this, and the boy would expend every ounce of nervous energy he had left.

Jason reflected on Josh's transformation. He was a changed man. In the final days leading up to the retrial, he hunkered down in his office and worked like someone who had put his mind, shoulders, and whole body to the task. He grew used to seeing him right before dawn, in the quasi-twilight before the workday officially began – hunching over legal documents in the fluorescent glow or cornering his team members with an arm around the shoulders, breaking down his thoughts and strategies. He began to think that only Josh could have dragged him out of that hole, as if he had taken that pendulum and turned it around as if he had thrown the world's burden onto his shoulders.

When the man on trial looked across the courtroom, the audience he saw was composed of those people who either directly or indirectly had shaped his life: there was Emma, with her eyes faded and empty from guilt, and Jamal, staring back at Jason through an expression choked with anger and despair, still clinging to hope that he would be found not guilty.

And Anita, sitting by Michael. The reminder that this was only the result of a genuinely hideous set of events, Anita was being held pending her legal proceedings, so she was sitting handcuffed with a pullover covering the metal restrainers.

His sister's eyes betrayed her, eliminating that old, confident self-possession that had carried her through the appeal three years earlier.

"I didn't want this to happen," Anita had told Michael. "I thought I was doing the right thing, but it was wrong. Someone should have stopped me."

But Michael was there too, shaking his head and looking around the room and sitting on his ass when he should be standing between Jason and those jurors. "Yes, Anita. You fucked it up, great times. But you were not the only one. No time to cry, now Let's try to make the wrong, right."

Josh had told Anita that he would do his best to ensure that the facts of this case would be heard and that Jason, the actual victim, would be given the justice he desperately sought.

Now, next to him, Josh felt the full force of that vow. The prosecution would not rest until Jason was back behind bars.

He also knew he had the truth and could count on everyone who believed Jason was innocent. And so, as the judge entered the courtroom and the bailiff screamed, "Call to order," Josh squared his shoulders and prepared for the fight, steeled to defend not just a client but now a friend.

The stage was set, and the actors gathered; Jason White needed to stand in the balance. As the first witness was sworn in and the retrial began to roll, the world waited with bated breath to see how this sordid saga might end.

## 43. Opening Statements

When the judge entered, all rose. Then, the judge called the case, sat on the bench, and looked around the room. The courtroom was quiet.

"Ladies and gentlemen of the jury – members of the public – for the trial of Jason White charged with the voluntary manslaughter of his father, Harry White. His Honour – the Stipendiary Magistrate on the first trial – convicted Mr White. Mr White was acquitted and, subsequently, released. But as new evidence had been discovered, the Court of Appeal has ordered a retrial." The judge started reading his papers.

"Recently, it has been brought to the attention of the public, the police and this Court that a document nullifies the evidence that led to the release of the respondent, who was brought back into custody pending this trial."

Judge Hawkins turned to the prosecution table. "Mr O'Connell, do you wish to make your opening statement to the court?"

The prosecutor, James O'Connell, a man in his sixties known in judiciary circles as a bully, stood up and smoothed down his jacket. He walked to the jury box, his stride firm and deliberate.

"Members of the jury, the prosecution will demonstrate – beyond a reasonable doubt – that Jason White has willingly murdered his father. By presenting you with evidence that the defendant had a conflicted relationship with his father and, on the date in question, murderously strove to kill Harry White with violent intent. By calling upon witnesses and submitting forensic scientific evidence, the prosecution will assure a conclusion wherein you will be forced – following your conscience – to convict the defendant of the aforementioned crime."

O'Connell sat down, and Judge Hawkins nodded to Silverman. "Mr Silverman, your opening statement, please."

Josh Silverman rose and approached the jury, his manner calm and assured.

"Members of the jury: I would like to call the court's attention to the fact that my client, Jason White, is not guilty. The evidence will show shortly that my client did not act out of free will but of years of abuse and trauma caused to him and his family by his father. Witnesses and experts will be presented to demonstrate the nature of the relationship into which my client has been thrust, one in which the family 'nurtured' his father's 'aggression and competitiveness'; this was also the manifestation of the legacy of chronic abuse that my client was a party to since birth. The defence will present evidence that my client's actions in the event of the crime leading to trial were those of a conflicted young man with no other option than to assert himself. Ultimately, the facts will demonstrate that the only just verdict is not guilty and the respondent be set free."

Josh returned to his seat, and Judge Hawkins addressed the court again.

"Thank you, counsellors. We will now proceed with the prosecution's first witness."

When Jason was called to the stand, he straightened in his chair. His heart thumped in his throat. He knew his life hung in the balance. The hope that had kept him alive until now felt vanishing.

## 44. *Jason*

The respondent took the stand. He rose, palms resting in his lap.

"Mr White," O'Connell began, his tone pointed and accusatory, "on 15 October of six years ago, you allegedly assaulted your father, a person named Harry White?"

Jason swallowed hard before answering. "Yes, that's correct."

"And during the confrontation, you punched your father and pushed him so forcefully that he hit his head on a table, ultimately killing him? Is that the allegation?"

"I ... I didn't mean to kill him. I didn't punch him; I just pushed him away."

Undeterred by Jason's emotion, O'Connell pressed on: "Mr White, you have had a longstanding conflict with your father, don't you? Isn't it true that you resented him and his efforts to control your life?"

"It was complex. I would never have hurt him," he replied haltingly.

The prosecutor was immune to any reason, but the prosecutor's questions were not: what O'Connell put before the jury was designed to portray the image of a petulant, resentful, angry, vindictive, then 20-year-old who, on a single explosive occasion, had chosen to manifest his vindictiveness with a particularly violent act, against his father.

O'Connell approached Jason again, holding up a copy of Anita's letter.

"Mr White," he asked, his eyes narrowing slightly. "Have you read this letter, written by your sister Anita?"

Jason nodded, his throat suddenly feeling dry. "Yes, I have."

"In this letter, your sister wrote that she lied the last time you went to trial and that she falsely accused your mother of murdering your father to protect you. What do you think?"

Jason's hands clenched around the lip of the witness stand. "I ... I don't know what to make of it. Anita and I had a falling out. I hadn't spoken to her in years."

O'Connell pushed on. "On its face, doesn't this letter contradicts everything you said throughout this proceeding? And doesn't it also contradict everything you have presented in any other judicial forum about being innocent of any and everything?"

"No, it's not. Every time I mentioned it, every time I spoke of this accident and my Dad's death, I said it was an accident. I thought it was an accident." Jason's voice wavered. "I said he slipped on the rug. It wasn't murder."

As O'Connell returned to his seat, Josh Silverman stood up and approached Jason, his demeanour gentle and understanding.

"Mr White," he said, in a light voice, "Jason, tell the court about your childhood and your father."

"My father was always very domineering and overbearing," Jason continued, pushing his spectacles further up his nose. "He was never satisfied with how well I was doing, and if I didn't meet his high expectations, he'd resort to abuse. He would hit me, my sister and my mother from time to time."

"And the night of the accident, what was going on with you and your Dad that made you fight with him?!" Josh nodded sympathetically.

"I'd just told him I'd quit my job. He thought I wouldn't survive, and he just had a go at me."

"Jason, did you intend to kill your father that night?"

"No, never," replied, choking up. "I couldn't kill my father. I loved him – yes, I loved him – even though he sometimes drove me crazy."

"Why did you keep Anita's letter? Some of what she wrote was either libellous or leave room to perjury."

Jason took a deep breath. "That letter, hateful as it was, was the last bridge I had with any family connection with my sister. I couldn't get rid of the letter."

"Why did you give that letter to Ms Emma Wilkins?"

"No, I... no way!" Jason said. "I didn't know that Emma had the letter. I thought it was, you know, I kept it in my flat. I thought it was private."

"So," confirmed Josh, "you're telling me that Emma had this letter, but you never told her that she had your permission to open it, let alone steal it."

"Yes," Jason confirmed with startled eyes. "She must have taken it from my flat after we split up. We didn't work out because of incompatibility, and I suppose she used the letter to avenge me."

Josh turned to the jury box.

"Ladies and gentlemen, I think it is now obvious that the appearance of this letter in the courtroom wasn't the doing of my client. If he were guilty, he would have destroyed that letter. He didn't. We will go into more detail about the latter as we continue our line of defence. Harry White did not die at the hands of my client. Jason White has maintained his innocence, and his friends, employer, charitable institutions, and therapist can testify that he's continued to be a fine citizen throughout the years he's been released."

Josh rested a reassuring hand on Jason's shoulder. "Thank you, Jason. No more questions, Your Honour."

When Josh finished questioning, the courtroom was abuzz with murmurs. All of a sudden, the case seemed both more complicated and more heartbreaking. Jason thought that perhaps the jury would see the letter for what it was: a horrible battleground in a broken family, not a death warrant.

Throughout, as Josh stood and retook his seat, he could see from the faces of the jurors how Jason's testimony was stretching their minds, how much messier than expected this trial, with its many greys in between the black-and-white of guilt and innocence, had turned out to be.

## 45. Anita

Anita's footsteps echoed in the hushed courtroom, the metallic clink of her handcuffs punctuating the silence. Her hands, visible beneath the loose sleeves of her sweater, trembled as she approached the witness stand. Josh stepped back as O'Connell, the prosecutor, addressed her first.

"Mrs. Trelawney," O'Connell blurted, "you made a statement, in a letter, to your brother Jason, that you had lied at his former trial; is that correct?"

Anita nodded, her voice shaking as she replied, "I didn't."

The prosecutor moved towards the witness with the copy of the letter.

"In this letter... did you write that it was your brother, not your mother, who killed your father?"

"I didn't," her eyes downcast.

Picking up where he left off, O'Connell picked up the copy of the letter. "Mrs. Trelawney, will you please read the part highlighted in the letter that concerns the court?"

Anita took a deep breath and began to read:

*Jason, I'm so sorry. You're out, free... but that's where it has to end for us, at the trial. I told them Mom killed Dad. But I don't even know if it was true. I thought I was right that I could protect Mom's memory, even if what I said wasn't entirely true. What I did, what she made me do... God forgive me. I hope that, in time, you can find peace and healing because I've lost any right to be part of that journey.*

When she finished reading, the court rustled with whispers. The prosecutor looked over at the jury. He was smiling.

So he asked: "Mrs. Trelawney, did you ever see Jason getting mad growing up?"

Anita shook her head. "No, he never," she said emphatically. "Jason was a sweet, gentle boy. The only violent human being in our household was my father."

The courtroom was quiet for a long few seconds. She swallowed hard, audibly.

"Ladies and gentlemen," O'Connell went on, "even the defendant's sister admits lying under oath. Someone in this trial is not telling the truth, which leaves little doubt regarding which side should win."

Josh Silverman then stood up and approached Anita, his expression gentle.

"Mrs. Trelawney," queried Josh, "your note seems to me to express some doubt about what occurred the night your father died. Would you say that this letter does not point to Jason's having been very much guilty or very much innocent?"

Anita nodded, swiping a rogue tear off her cheek. "Yes, that's right. I was sleeping when everything happened, and I was emotionally raw, as my mother had died recently, when I wrote that letter in this very Courthouse and, as a result, it does reflect my feelings of doubt and regret – but no matter what I said, what I believed then and now doesn't change the fact that Jason and my father were alone in that room that night and except for Jason, nobody knows what happened."

Josh turned to the jury. "So, ladies and gentlemen, while those words are heartfelt and complex, they don't answer the fundamental question of this case, which is: Did Jason White mean to kill his father?"

"Would you confirm that your deceased mother, Germaine White, confided that she had finisher your father and that since his death, the two of you had found peace at home without him abusing you? Member of the jury, we have some letters from the witness sent to his borther, while in jail, confirming what I stated."

"I do. If we missed anyone, at home, this was Jason, not my abusive father."

"I have no further quest..."

Anita interrupted Josh.

"There's something I've never told anybody, not even my husband." The courtroom went silent.

"When I was 7 years old, my Dad... he raped me," she openly declared with a whisper of a voice. "I told my mum about it, and then she took us from that house to a shelter. I was too young to comprehend what was happening then, fully, but as time went on, I realised how his violence changed our family."

The murmurs and gasps escaped across the courtroom. Jason looked at his sister, and tears and shock flushed his face. The judge banged his gavel for order.

"Given this new information," he said, "I think it best to adjourn for today. Court tomorrow morning."

When the bailiff's grip made Anita leave the courtroom, Jason was still sitting there, looking shellshocked and confused by the news his sister had just revealed. The jury, dipping in sympathy and horror, stared back.

Josh rested his hand reassuringly on Jason's shoulder. "We'll get there, we'll get through this," he said. "The truth will come out."

He barely heard him as his mind back-flipped and loop-the-looped over the many years of pain that his family had suffered – far worse, he now knew, than he had ever imagined.

## 46. *The Social Services Files*

In the wake of Anita's bombshell, Josh and Michael hoped that the new subpoena would force social services to reveal yet more of the White family file and, therein, discover the smoking gun: declarations Germaine White had made regarding the abuse she had reported to social services. They believed that these would prove invaluable to Jason because they would have shown Anita's frailty, and her letter would have been justified from many points of view. A need to break with the past was the main thing.

They finally went to the social services office to get the files. At first, the staff refused, citing confidentiality and the controversial nature of the documents, not to mention that no manager was available to read the subpoena. Then, perceiving the high-profile nature of the case, let alone its potential influence on the trial, the social services worker let Josh have the files he wanted.

As the two lawyers read through the documents, they noticed a record of one of the nights Germaine had gone with her two children to the shelter – and, as they had suspected, there was no mention of the sexual violence Anita had experienced: Germaine did say that she *felt threatened tonight*.

Now this – *the bugger might have done to me just about anything, but now, he has outdone all abominations!*

These words hung in the air, and there was the possibility of what Harry might have done to his daughter, irritating their pores and sending a chill between them. She had not directly accused him, yet the social worker made a poignant addition in writing:

*Perhaps the child? She seems too quiet for someone her age.*

The longer Josh and Michael read, the more their hearts sank: the files were a deposition and description of a family in turmoil, a mother warding off the monster in her own home and trying to keep the children of her house safe.

The shock proved cruel for Michael because he had known Harry for years. He knew the couple well, yet he felt there must have been a way to stop it and was clueless. He felt betrayed, angry, appalled, and tormented with guilt. "God, I would have done so much more if I had known. If I had known, I would have ended it myself."

The two walked out of the social services office with file folders, promising justice for Jason, Anita, and Germaine.

Back at the office, they considered how to proceed and what additional evidence they would present in court. They would have to be extra careful now: they needed to push for justice while protecting Anita and respecting Germaine's memory.

## 47. Emma

When the court reconvened the next day before any testimony was taken, the judge addressed the room in an imposing tone at an imposing decibel; he said that "all parties had agreed, including the prosecution and the defence, that the testimonies would be heard as previously planned; as to the new evidence" that the defence "would be presenting, they would argue over it after the witnesses were called." He would listen and decide, but it would go forward for now. He then stood up and signalled for the next witness to be called.

The prosecutor, O'Connell, stood up, buttoning his jacket as he walked to the witness stand: "The prosecution calls Ms Emma Wilkins to the stand."

She approached the stand, ambling, her face unreadable. She was sworn in, and the Crown prosecutor started questioning her.

"Ms Wilkins, please tell us about your relationship with the defendant, Jason White."

She glanced at Jason, then answered. "We were in love for a while."

O'Connell nodded, and a glimmer of a smile played at the corners of his mouth. "And, from what you've said, would you say your feelings for Mr White were unusual? A bit, I don't know, fascinated or even obsessed?"

Emma shifted in her seat. "Yes, I did. But I wouldn't say I obsessed over him."

"So, Ms Wilkins," he continued, "Why did it end?"

"We had our differences," Emma replied, her voice strained. "It just didn't work out."

"Would you say that you felt... scorned? And you wanted revenge?"

"No, I left him. If anyone should have felt scorned, this was Mr White, not me."

As O'Connell concluded his questioning, Josh Silverman approached the witness stand, his expression serious.

"Ms Wilkins, I would ask you to look at that letter written by Anita White, the defendant's sister. How did you come to have that letter?"

She hesitated, her gaze darting around the room. "I... I found it."

Josh's brow furrowed. "Found it where exactly?"

"In Jason's apartment," she admitted, her voice barely above a whisper.

"And why, if you found this letter, which may well have contained damning evidence, why did you not go straight to the police?"

Emma thought for a minute, and then, finally, "I... I don't know."

Josh faced the judge and said: "Your Honour, I question the relevance of this witness's testimony. Despite being under oath, Ms Wilkins is unable or unwilling to give straight answers to our questions. Ms Wilkins has reopened this case and is not telling us much."

The judge gave her a look of dismay. "Ms Wilkins, you are under oath. That means you must comply with the law to answer the questions formulated for you insofar as your conscience and mind allow you to. Failing to do so might cause you to face some charges yourself. I am sure you will take this warning as seriously as you should."

Emma nodded, her face white and her hands shaking. And then she tried to speak, but before she got a single word out of her, her eyes rolled up, and her head lolled forward into her lap.

Wailing, she collapsed from the stand, her body sliding down to the court floor. There was an audible gasp and a murmur from the audience as the bailiff rushed to her side to check for a pulse.

Josh looked at O'Connell. The prosecutor looked back at him. Their faces were tired and puzzled. "Order." The judge's voice soared over things.

"We'll take a short break while the witness is attended to, medically," he announced, sweeping his gaze over the room. "The court will reconvene in one hour."

When the courtroom cleared, Josh felt that Emma's fainting fit was not an accident. He knew the letter held the key to Jason's fate, which was in her hands. But with her faint, the key slipped further from their grasp.

A thought. A quick one. He was determined to get Emma to confess. Everything.

She reappeared an hour later, paler but poised. Sucking in her breath, she said to the court: "I apologise for what happened; it will not happen again."

The judge nodded. "Ms Wilkins, you are still under oath. It would be best if you answered truthfully," he reiterated.

Josh Silverman went to Emma again. "Ms Wilkins, back to the initial question, why did you take the letter from my client's flat – why did you rob him of it?"

She paused before replying: "The letter must have been mistakenly in a book I took – I realised this after opening the volume. The news gave me renewed bitterness."

"And this resentment led you to broadcast the letter's contents?" Josh pressed.

"Yes," she admitted, her voice barely audible.

Josh's face tightened. "This broadcast made you a lot of money, didn't it?"

She shifted uncomfortably in her seat. "I suppose so, yes."

"So, can we say that your hate for Jason led you to act as you did instead of going to the police? I don't think we need any answer to that. One final question, Miss Wilkins. Have you ever been diagnosed with hybristophilia?"

"No, I haven't," she replied, her tone defensive.

Josh fished something from his briefcase: "My Lord, look what I got here! I have a report from the therapist who treated Ms Wilkins – and it states categorically that she was suffering from a paraphilia at the time these events occurred and that paraphilia is hybristophilia."

"Your Honour," Josh added, looking at the judge, "these documents are available because the therapist in question thought that Ms Wilkins was a potential danger to herself and the others, so no confidentiality between the therapist and the patient has been broken."

The courtroom hummed quietly, and Josh slipped the report into the judge's hands. Emma blushed with fury, her eyes flashing as she stared at Jason.

"You sonofabitch," she yelled. "You ruined my life! What if you'd stayed in prison?"

The judge banged his gavel, his voice booming over the din. "Ms Wilkins, you will be quiet or held in contempt of this court!" He gestured angrily to the bailiff. "Bring the witness down from the stand and have her placed in a holding cell until I can rule on whether she can continue to behave in this manner."

As they escorted her offstage, still screaming at Jason, Josh returned to his chair, with a grin on his face. He knew that Emma's tantrum and revelation of her psychological history would do more to discredit her and her motivations than anything he could have said. The idea that he had to discredit her with lies about Michael's fees was no longer needed.

With a resigned tone, the judge addressed the court: "For this testimony and the new evidence brought forward, the court stands adjourned for the day. The court will reconvene tomorrow at 9 am and hear prosecution and defence arguments on the admissibility of the therapist's report and the relevance to these proceedings."

## 48. *Jamal*

Josh Silverman walked the short distance to the witness stand, where Jamal sat nervously, hands clasped in his lap. Josh flashed him a reassuring smile.

"Mr Adams, can you tell the court what kind of relationship you had with the defendant, Jason White?"

Jamal swallowed, his voice hoarse: "I've been a Jason supporter from day one, ever since his first trial. I followed his case because I believed in his innocence. I developed these feelings toward him over the years, and we began writing letters to each other."

Josh nodded. "Yeah, and did Jason ever talk to you at all about how his Dad died or what it was like, you know, for his family?"

"Not in great detail," the witness replied. "But he did say that he felt bad about what happened and that his father's death had been an accident, and also that he and his family had often been abused, physically and psychologically, by his father. I have all the letters we exchanged here with me, if needed."

"Thank you, Mr Adams, no need for the time being," replied Josh. His voice was gentle. "I would like to turn to Emma Wilkins. In dealing with her, did you ever come across any tendencies to suggest that a desire for publicity or financial gain may have driven her?"

There was a pause before Jamal said: "I wasn't sure. Emma always struck me as more interested in the publicity surrounding Jason's case than Jason himself. But then, when she started to cash in on his letters and use his life story to her advantage, I stopped reading her."

Josh spoke up to the jury. "I believe, Your Honour, that Mr Adams' testimony speaks to the disposition of Emma Wilkins and the actual motivations for her conduct in this matter."

As Josh returned to his seat, James O'Connell rose to begin his cross-examination.

"Mr Adams," O'Connell said, his tone sharply accusatory, "do you not feel that you have become a little infatuated with that young man—that you feel toward him something more than friendship—or support further than fraternal?"

Jamal turned serious and squirmed in his seat. "I care about Jason, but it's – I don't know – not an obsession."

O'Connell wasn't giving up. "And yet – you've written all these letters to him, saying that you're his *Yes Minion*, his *robot*, his *maid*, his *wife*. And you've created websites and online communities for him and his case. Isn't that a little bit beyond normal, healthy interest?"

"I was just trying to help someone I thought was worthy." The words came out shaky from his mouth. "Someone that I thought was denied justice."

"Or maybe," suggested O'Connell, slightly sharp in his sarcasm, "you were fishing, trying to find validation and attention for yourself just like Emma Wilkins, and maybe you saw Jason White as a way to gratify your lack, no matter what his true situation happened to be."

"No, that isn't right!" shouted Jamal, his eyes welling with tears. "I like Jason. He is a good person. I would never take advantage like that."

O'Connell shrugged, and his lips curled into something resembling a smirk. "Of course, he wouldn't, Your Honour. No further questions."

As Jamal dropped his eyes to the floor and stepped off the witness stand, his shoulders hunched and his face sagged, Josh felt sympathy for the young man. His testimony revealed some of Emma's background, but more than that, it showed the depths of Jamal's feelings in the case, if not his paraphilia.

Josh knew the jury would have to chisel away at Jamal's utterances, drawing out the internal truth from the dense nest of feelings and fixations that had grown up around Jason White. It was a tough job, but it might make the difference between that trial's outcome and the very life of the young man at its heart.

## 49. Michael

Now that Jamal had finished his testimony, it was time for Josh Silverman to call his next witness. "The defence calls Mr Michael Jones to the stand."

Michael took the stand, his eyes downcast and his head held high. He took the oath and sat down. He stared at Josh.

"Mr Jones," Josh continued, "would you please tell this court about your relationship with the White family and, concerning the defendant, Jason White?"

Michael cleared his throat and spoke in a level voice. "I am a long-time friend and personal legal advisor to the White family. I have known Jason since birth; I have been close to both parents and represented all three in various court matters. I am also Jason's godfather."

Josh nodded. "As you developed this relationship with the family – were you ever suspicious that bad things were happening within the home?"

Michael's face twisted in pain. "I had my suspicions, don't get me wrong. I noticed the bruises on Germaine and the children behaving oddly, but there was no concrete evidence – and she always insisted everything was fine."

"But that changed, didn't it?" Josh prompted gently.

Michael drew in a long breath, tears trembling in his eyes. "Yes. She told me just before the appeal. She said that, on the night Harry died, after Jason had pushed him, she ... she finished the job. She killed Harry to protect the children from more abuse."

There was an audible gasp in the courtroom, and the judge banged the gavel for order and quiet. Josh waited for the murmuring to subside before he continued.

"And what did you do with this information, Mr. Jones?"

"Nothing. I kept to myself. I was Jason's lawyer and felt our evidence was enough. I wanted to spare the family from further pain and having to give up the case."

As Josh concluded his questioning, O'Connell approached the stand, his expression sceptical.

"Mr Jones, if you are to be believed, then you denied the court this critical evidence in Jason White's first trial. You allowed an innocent man to go to prison for a crime he didn't commit."

Michael's shoulders sagged, and he shook the head side to side, "Yes, I did, but not in the first trial. I found out about it just before the appeal. However, I don't think my guilt will ever lessen. I'm stuck with it for the rest of my days. If it's redemption I'm looking for, I won't find it here. But what I am doing, I believe, is doing the right thing."

O'Connell frowned. "And you expect us to believe you? You have no evidence. No proof. It's been how many years? And now is when you decide to tell us?"

"I have no obligation to you. I have no reason to lie. Germaine was my best friend, and Jason is like my son. I failed Germaine and Jason because I didn't speak up when I should have, and I'm not going to fail them now by lying."

The CP rolled his eyes. "Well, that's very convenient for you, Mr Jones, isn't it?" he said with a dismissive chuckle. "A deathbed confession that you alone were present for, and only you were told at the eleventh hour. A nice little story, that."

As he walked back to his seat, his testimony still hovering over the courtroom, Josh knew that the jury would have to decide whether to believe his version of Germaine's confession.

Josh glanced at Jason. His gaze filled with uncertainty and hope. To Josh, it seemed his fate was floating there, like a twig on the surface of this vast pool of concealments and deceptions. His fate rested on the whim of a jury.

## 50. *The Verdict*

During the trial, the court also heard testimony from several witnesses about Jason's personality and mental state since being released from prison.

Jason's boss at the warehouse was the one of the witnesses to be called to the stand. He testified that Jason was a terrific worker and a natural leader, someone who had become a role model in his eyes. "Jason's been an exceptional employee," he confirmed. "He's responsible, reliable, highly productive. I've never had any doubt about his behaviour or mental state. He inspires confidence and is admired by his colleagues."

Afterwards, a helper from the charity where Jason had worked. How Jason had been dedicated to improving the lives of disadvantaged children; about how Jason had awoken the children to their own lives – in one of many retellings of his life story – of pluck, courage, upward thrust; about how the kids had looked up to him as they looked up to the staircase leading them from the dull basement to the colourful light above; about his hesitant remarks; his surprise at being addressed; and, then, how he'd begun to tell the assembled young ones about the times when things had been challenging. "Kids," he would say, "there's nothing you can be going through that I didn't go through worse. We've all tasted the bitter side of life, and yet, somehow, none of us died. We are all still here. Can you repeat that for the people at the back?"

Jason's therapist, Dr Carl Adamson, took the stand to explain his patient's mental illness. He testified that Jason had made great strides in his healing over the past several years, and although he still had trouble with some PTSD symptoms, he was largely stabilised. "Jason has made a great deal of progress in accepting the dysfunction and abuse he grew up with and learning to live with his parents' deaths and learning about, especially, his mother's actions," Dr Adamson continued. "He has worked extremely hard to overcome the guilt and grief and other emotions by learning healthy ways to cope and has developed a good support system. He has deflected those negative influences and allure coming from his fans and understood that his life is not the one his paraphiliac admirers think it is."

The judge ruled the reports relating to Emma's paraphilia would not be admitted to the official court record because they were not relevant to the legal question before the Court as to Jason's guilt or innocence. However, he did permit the social services report of the sexual abuse undergone by Anita at the hands of the her father. This was vital in creating a picture of the abusive and violent background from which the events of 15 October had emerged.

At the end of the trial, the prosecution and defence provided their closing arguments. The CP contended that Anita's letter must be given great weight since it undermined Jason's account and supported a pattern of deception in the family. The prosecution urged the jury to entertain the possibility that Jason had murdered his father and that his mother had taken the fall for him. He recommended confirming the voluntary manslaughter charges and that the respondent should be sent back to jail to fulfil his sentence.

The defence endeavoured to present the letter as an emotional outpouring from a traumatised young woman struggling to reconcile the loss of her parents and the tortured legacy of abuse. Without proof that Jason premeditated his acts of violence, arguments that he had grown into an exemplary citizen since his release served to demonstrate the truth of his character. "Jason White is not a murderer," announced Josh Silverman in his summation. "He is a survivor of horrors that many of us cannot even begin to imagine, who had to rise from the ashes and rebuild his life, and went from the dark cloud of abuse to someone who has brightened the world for those around him. The tragedy of what happened to the White family cannot be undone, but we can ensure that justice is served and an innocent man will not be sacrificed to someone else's sin."

When the jury was dismissed to consider their verdict, the charged atmosphere gave way to palpable silence as each member filed out of the court. Jason remained seated at the defence table, his eyes closed, fingertips pressed together in front of him. It was now in the hands of 12 strangers who had spent only a few weeks sorting through lies and secrets that 'the Whites had been guarding against each other for decades.'

But whatever it would yield, for the first time in years, the truth had a real prospect of setting Jason free so he could finally begin building a future without the ghosts of his past. He will have to rebuild his rapport with Anita and, most importantly, get all the help he could to overcome the terrible revelations that happened during this trial.

The courtroom swelled to a standing-room-only brim as the jurors returned through the rear doors, their sunken countenances betraying nothing. The defendant sat unmoving, his chest trembling beneath the crisp vest of his navy blazer—his pulse racing—as he awaited the verdict that would seal his fate.

"Order in court." The judge tapped the gavel. "Has the jury reached a verdict?" he asked, looking at the foreman.

The foreman, a neat and silver-haired man in his fifties, folded the poorly stapled papers he had been distributing and cleared his throat. "We have, Your Honour."

"Please read the verdict."

The foreman forked his glasses, lifted a slip of paper, and began reading. "We, the jury, in the case of The Crown versus Jason White, on the charge of voluntary manslaughter ... find the defendant ... not guilty."

At that moment, as a wave of gasps and murmurs swept across the courtroom and Jason's supporters erupted into sobs and applause, Josh Silverman clapped a hand on his client's shoulder and broke into a smile.

With that, the judge banged his gavel and demanded: "Mr. Foreman, please explain the jury's reasoning behind this verdict?"

"Yes, Your Honour," said the foreman. "After hearing all the evidence, we determined that we had reasonable doubt as to whether Jason White actuated the felonious intent to kill his father. Mrs. Trelawney's emotional testimony left some unanswered questions regarding Jason's guilt. Still, the reports from social services indicated that Jason and his family suffered years of abuse and trauma at the hands of Harry White. This context is important."

He paused and glanced at Jason and the judge. "Moreover, the account from Jason's employer, the charity worker, and his psychotherapist all speak to his good character and the extent to which he has rehabilitated himself since being released."

And the foreman looked Jason in the face. "While we realise the terrible suffering and loss that the White family has suffered, we do not believe justice would be served by condemning the defendant for an act that he did not intend to commit and, with this verdict, we hope that he can put the tragedy behind him and move forward with his life at last."

When the judge thanked the jury for their service and dismissed them, Jason sat stunned, tears flowing freely. He had dared hope, but hearing the word 'not guilty' felt more like a dream from which he might wake up at any moment.

Josh Silverman threw his arms around him in a big bear hug, his eyes welling up with tears. "You did it, Jason," he choked out. "You stuck up for what was right, and the jury saw it that way. I'm so proud of you."

"Thank you, Josh." And while he was thanking him, Michael and Jamal approached him. Michael was crying like a baby, while Jamal was glowing. Jason, irrationally, ignored Michael completely and hugged his biggest fan so tight that the big guy had to ask him to release him. They all laughed. Jason looked Jamal in the eye. "Thank you, my friend. Thank you for staying by me all the way." The friend hugged him again, "OK, but now? What about a kiss?" Jason kissed him on the lips. Everyone cheered. "But don't get used to it!" Jason warned.

When the situation returned to normal, and Jason went to complete the paperwork, he was thoughtful. He thought of his mother and Anita—the family he had lost and those secrets that had torn it apart. He knew that scars would last for the rest of his life, but finally, he felt like he could have a future.

Free again, he knew that this journey would be long and arduous. He had people who believed in him and stood by him over his most brutally challenging years. He made new friends but, sadly, lost some old ones.

Then he walked out of his shadow and into the sunshine, and whatever the future held was up to him – he had won his acquittal, and now he had to make a life worthy of that victory.

# Part 7 – The Epilogue

The dust was starting to settle after Jason White's tumultuous trial. The lives of those somehow connected to the man who became infamous were moving forward with the revelations in the courtroom.

The revelation of her paraphilia and the horrific treatment of Jason provided a turning point for Emma Wilkins. Under the brutal eye of the public and abandoned by the people who once adored her, she had to face the ugly hunger that motivated her actions. Running low on money and with her online history all but wiped clean, she hit a fork in the road: she could not go on with obsessive behaviour with manipulation.

So much so that she decided to make amends for her past and try to find a healthier future by seeing a therapist, again. In intense therapy, she started to untangle the web of her traumas and how they played out in some creepy connection to Jason. She was in the slow process of not only finding a new sense of self but could now, through having so much self-awe under her belt, have a new kind of empathy for those who suffered from similar brain weaselling and began to build a new life from this place of genuine understanding with a desire to give back to others.

As she evolved within her healing journey, she shifted her focus to advocating and speaking out about mental health and standing up for those who have been abused or exploited. That led to her volunteering at a local crisis centre, sharing her voice and story with those who needed her most. Eventually, she worked up the courage even to write about them, hoping that by telling her own story — her road to healing and recovery — she could help others come to terms with their demons and find a way out of the cycle of trauma and obsession.

Her first book was a best-seller.

The events of the trial altered Jamal Adams as well.

He was finally inspired to find his path after being by Jason's side during some of his lowest moments. Moved by Jason's plight and the strength of their bond, he felt compelled to draw from his own experiences and passions and set out on a new mission — founding a non-profit to aid those who, like Jason, had been wrongly convicted and needed help getting back on their feet once free. Inspired by his hero and buoyed by his financial backing, he set out on his new mission to help draw attention to the errors within the English criminal justice system and the huge economic and personal toll of getting it completely wrong.

As a Reform Advocate, he went to conferences, he went to protests, he went to talk to lawmakers left and right to make sure no kid would have to end up in a place the way Jason did. He evolved and built his supporters who believed in justice and equality as he did. One was Tariq, an activist like him and an old university friend who helped him navigate his identity and family problems, before everything happened. Over time, as they laboured side by side, Jamal and Tariq's friendship transformed into love, their activism and mutual encouragement the solid bedrock on which they built their relationship.

The trial was a wake-up call for Michael Jones, a red flag signalling the ethical trade-offs he had sometimes made to protect Jason and the White family.

He could no longer continue to practice law as he had, haunted by his complicity in Jason's wrongful conviction. In the months after the trial, he took the hard step of leaving his high-power law firm and turning his life over to a new mission: to help the innocent by stepping into the criminal justice system with his sleeves rolled up. He fought challenging pro-bono cases to free people who had been wrongfully incarcerated. He turned to the guidance he had learned from the White case and his own mistakes on these new pathways.

He pressured aggressively for transparency and accountability in the court, railing against the unseemly deals and unwritten rules that had buried Germaine's admission for all these years. He was reminded of a way to right the wrong in his work, though there was no way he could; through his work, he could take the rest of his life to ensure others were not hurt as the people he broke. By doing so, he would deepen relationships with his peers, as with Josh Silverman, who would become a cherished comrade in arms in the battle for justice.

For his part, the trial was a bittersweet end to the capricious winds that had swirled around Jason White in the months after that. He was relieved once the several years of legal battles no longer dominated his life, but he also knew more profoundly that the scars the White family history had left on him would linger for a long time.

Beyond telling the world Jason was not guilty, Beyond helped him carve out a new life. One of Jason's dearest friends, Josh Silverman, was a man whose untiring efforts had played a crucial part in his release. Silverman regularly visited Ealing to meet with Jason and track down any possible miscarriage of justice. The two would frequently go out for a drink or dinner, ranging from more lowbrow discussions to the loftier conversations they often engaged in after those drinks. Over his seemingly tireless efforts to uncover the truth regarding the case, Josh had won Jason's trust as a steadfast defender of integrity and justice. Hopefully, long after the echo of the trial had dimmed, their friendship would continue. And, by the way, they did visit that new cocktail bar in Brixton. Only once. They disliked it.

In the weeks and months after his release, Jason had still to deal with grief at the death of his mother, the revelation of her complicity in the murder of his father and the extent of the abuse his sister had faced at the hands of Harry White. However, even at his lowest, he believed there were more close friends and family, and he could not endure his fears alone. He rediscovered new meaning in his mission working with an organisation he chose to be involved with when locked up, sharing his life story to give hope and healing to others who had gone through hardships, 'just like I did.' Over the years, Jason was able to start rebuilding a new life for himself slowly. He had to dig deep into the painful past and into the reasons never to allow a return to the abusive pattern that had haunted his family for as long as he could remember.

With Anita, they coped by finding ways to celebrate their mother's memory and forgive her for whatever choices she might have made under unthinkable circumstances and fear. Moreover, between them all, Jason clung to what his tortuous experience had taught him about what it meant to endure, what it was to be kind and patient, and the substance of the love and friendship that had gotten him through his most helpless times.

His past scars would never leave him; they would forever be a painful reminder of the path he had followed through the dark to see the light again. He also knew that wasn't true, that he was far from alone in his decision, and that he was supported by those who had chosen to stick by him, as well as the fortitude and bravery to tackle whatever came next.

As a result of the trial, Anita Trelawney was cleared of any wrongdoing, and she went back to live happily with her husband, Glenn, and their small boy, Henry, in the home at St Ives. Her past scars may never truly heal, but they were alleviated by her family and the knowledge that her brother was finally free from the bondage of the terrible events that had corrupted his life – and hers.

And here, on an October afternoon in Cornwall, was Jason, his feet planted on the windy cliffside overlooking the sea. Anita was standing beside him, her hand resting on his arm.

"I can't believe we're here, you know," he yelled over the wind. "After all this time, I can't believe it's real."

She appeared to be in disbelief, her eyes wet with unfallen tears. "But it's real, brother. You're free, and we're together. That's all that matters now."

He nodded, his throat tightening. "But think of Mum and Dad and all the lies that kept our family together for years. It was wrong. I wish we would have been different."

"The past is the past," reassured him, Anita. "They're dead, and we cannot change that." Then, in a voice low and full of quiet sadness, full of the beginnings: "All we can do is live the life and love. We can stop that abuse from spreading and traumatising others. We can honour our mother by touching any of those beautiful children in the world and letting our hope spring forth."

Turning to her, Jason was still smiling, but now his eyes were filled with gratitude and determination. "You're right; we have another chance. I want to keep paying it forward. I want to keep making a difference to other kids like us."

She hugged him close, his ear boxed against her shoulder. "You are already, Jase, how you've dealt with everything. I wish Mum could have seen the man you've become. I'm very proud of you."

They were standing on the edge of the world, hanging on to each other, and the world suddenly felt more peace than he'd had in years. He would always carry the ghosts, his ghosts, with him, but they didn't have to be the face anymore because he'd fought for what felt like the truth in his life, and fighting had shown him how to create a new reality – to say yes to hope, healing, love, and family.

The sun was setting, and the sky turned orange and gold. Jason and Anita turned again on their feet and returned to the two-story cottage, where Glenn and Henry waited, ready with the fireplace and supper.

Ultimately, that was the absolute legacy of the White family; it was not the pain and grief that strived to engulf them but love, which fortified them, and the attributes of a survivor mentality that pushed everyone to rise as kin through redemptive clouds.

Anita, looked at him, and whispered, "Ya... Right here is your home... in all the ways."

And Jason, for the first time in his life, was free.

AND THAT'S MY VERSION of Jason White's story. I was there at the start, his mate, his confidant. When he needed me most, I let him down. I left him alone that night for a fleeting pleasure... I'll carry this sense of guilt as a weight on my soul.

Forever.

# THE END

# Author's Notes: The Seductive Dangers of Hybristophilia

Throughout this narrative, you were immersed in the dark psychological underpinnings of hybristophilia - the sexual and emotional attraction to those who commit criminal acts. While fictional, the manifestations portrayed rang alarmingly true to this little-understood paraphilic disorder.

We saw the roots of Emma Wilkins' obsession reflect what Paul Fedoroff, director of Sexual Behaviours Clinic in Ottawa, describes as the "outlaw mystique" that can erotically draw people to criminals (Schmid, 2005). Her fixation escalated in ways mirroring documented cases of hybristophilic stalkers exploiting their targets for money and attention (Purcell et al., 2004).

Jamal Adams exemplified symbolic hybristophilia, where attraction fixates on the criminal's celebrity persona rather than any real intimacy (Money, 1986). Cut off from genuinely knowing Jason, Jamal idealised his narrative into a delusional fantasy relationship.

At its most unnerving, Michael Jones' unethical enabling of Jason's imprisonment hints at a subset of hybristophiles who unconsciously facilitate criminal acts to create their desired object of attraction (Roof et al., 1997).

Nevertheless, there is hope that the cycle can be broken. Emma's arc aligns with cognitive-behavioural therapy principles, helping hybristophiles recontextualise sexual scripts (Akerman &

Beech, 2012). Jamal's turn to advocacy reflects restoring self-worth through positive experiences.

The psychological realities underlying hybristophilia are distressing, but achievable enlightenment exists for those willing to confront their darkest impulses. May this exploration illuminate a disturbing human proclivity while illuminating a path toward healing.

# References

Akerman, G., & Beech, A.R. (2012). A systematic review of measures of deviant sexual interest and arousal. Psychiatry, Psychology and Law, 19(1), 118-143.

Money, J. (1986). Lovemaps: Clinical concepts of sexual/erotic health and pathology, paraphilia, and gender transposition. Irvington Publishers.

Purcell, R., Pathé, M., & Mullen, P.E. (2004). When do repeated intrusions become stalking? Journal of Forensic Psychiatry & Psychology, 15(4), 571-583.

Roof, P.R., Hansen, H., & Dietz, P. (1997). Hybristophilia and sexual charges: A follow-up study. Journal of Forensic Sciences, 42(3), 602-603.

Schmid, D. (2005). Natural Born Celebrities: Serial Killers in American Culture. University of Chicago Press.

[1] RD Laing's Observations of an Aleutian Tractor (1964).

[2] the failed silent movie star from Sunset Boulevard (1950), deluded by her reality-defying fragments of 'recollection'.

# About The Author

## Luigi Pascal Rondanini

Author also writes as Pascal De Napoli.

Luigi Pascal Rondanini's determination and tenacity in pursuing his ideals pushed him to leave his native Naples to pursue the opportunities offered by the world.

Born in November 1967 and raised in the capital of Campania, from a young age he cultivated a passion for writing and politics.

The desire for social justice led him to actively engage in social issues and write literary works inspired by these values.

At a very young age, he moved abroad to the United Kingdom, where he embarked on a brilliant career in the financial sector and continued his passion for writing, infusing his works with social and political themes with courage and frankness.

Despite living in London, Rondanini has never lost the connection with his Neapolitan roots after having lived on five continents. In his writings, Neapolitan culture and identity emerge vividly as an example of cultural diversity that enriches humanity.

Rondanini wants to inspire readers to pursue their dreams with courage and determination. His story demonstrates how, with commitment and sacrifice, you can achieve great goals while remaining true to yourself and your values.

Rondanini is also a narrator and an Audiobook publisher for other authors.

Contact him at www.rondanini.com[1]

---

1. http://www.rondanini.com

# Books By This Author

Vanished Echoes: A Breaking News Story

A Week of Shadows and Light: A Journey Through Grief and Hope

Bridging Worlds: Stories of Connection Across Time and Space

Discovering Wonder: Seeing the World Through a Child's Eyes

I Fantasmi del Passato: Storie di amicizia, tradimenti e bugie non dette (Italian Edition)

Pazzigno A/R: I Fantasmi del Passato (Italian Edition)

The Ghosts of the Past: A Story of friendship, betrayal and unspoken lies

Politics for Young Minds

Economics for Young Minds

Project Management for Young Minds

The Tales to Grow by Collection: Tales to Grow by, A Whale's Mercy and Light Within in one inspirational volume

Reimagined Tales: Subverting Expectations in Fantasy and Digital Legends

# Don't miss out!

Visit the website below and you can sign up to receive emails whenever Luigi Pascal Rondanini publishes a new book. There's no charge and no obligation.

https://books2read.com/r/B-A-AAPAB-ZJCCF

BOOKS 2 READ

Connecting independent readers to independent writers.

Milton Keynes UK
Ingram Content Group UK Ltd.
UKHW020010061124
450708UK00001B/74